October 15th, 1877 (Monday) – Henry Flagler moves to Jacksonville

January 22nd, 1912 (Monday) – The railroad is completed

August 30th, 1935 (Friday) – 3 days prior to the Labor Day Hurricane's landfall

September 2nd, 1935 (Monday) – Landfall of the Labor Day Hurricane

September 4th, 1935 (Friday) – Completion of trip for last ever Overseas Railroad passengers

November 14th, 1937 (Sunday) – Dedication of the Labor Day Hurricane monument over two years after its landfall

The Final Run of Flagler's Folly

Prelude

September 2nd, 1995

The older couple stepped out from the cold air-conditioned comfort of their car into the oppressive heat of the mid-day sun. The gentleman waited at the front corner of the bumper of the sleek, black Mercedes as his wife walked slowly around to slide her hand into his.

They had done well for themselves over the years, but more importantly, they were here, and they were happy just being together. He was slim, not bad looking and just under 6 feet, but still not athletic. Although these days, his lack of athleticism didn't seem to matter as much to him anymore. She was still attractive, way out of his league, or so he always said, and had not lost any of her grace. But as they walked towards the monument, the pain and grief from so many years ago was still readily written all over their bearing as their feet crunched and shifted unsteadily on the small, white stones beneath their shoes.

It was 60 years ago, and yet, it felt like so much less than that. The wounds were still there, just not as raw as they once had been. But still not completely healed either.

They had tried to stop by every year and leave flowers, but sometimes life just got in the way. She felt much guiltier about it than he did, but she assumed that was just the stronger feminine empathy within her. And he did feel guilty when they missed their annual ritual, just not as much as she did. Just like on that fateful day. It hurt her so much more than it did him. That was just how she had always been.

Sadly, there were even a few times when a couple of years would pass before they would be able to get back to perform their duties. But even when that was the case, their loved ones were never far from their thoughts.

Letting go of her husband's hand as they rounded the corner to the southernmost side of the monument, the stately woman walked silently by herself up to the large structure and placed the flowers gently in front of it on the beautiful, polished, reflective stone. There was a spot on the other side of the monument to put flowers, but she had always preferred to place them directly in front of the stone monolith.

Both of her friend's names were inscribed on the plaque, just on the other side of the monument. She had seen the names written there once before a couple of years after the hurricane, but since then... Well, she just couldn't bring herself to go around to that side of the monument again. Their names were barely legible etched as they were in the marble, but she knew that they were there. His was listed as cremated and hers was listed only as "missing."

But on the card that was stuck into the flowers, her friend's names were written in very precise, detailed and attractive cursive script, just as they were every year that she dropped flowers off in their remembrance.

Her husband stood back, quietly giving her room to express her grief in her own way. Meanwhile, his thoughts, as he was sure hers did too, drifted back to that ugly, fateful weekend. He shivered slightly as his mind dredged up the old memories. There had been a slight bit of a breeze that had passed by them at that moment, but with the oppressive heat of the island today, he knew it was not the wind that was giving him chills at that moment. His friends had been young and foolish at that time, but they certainly did not deserve that.

He glanced up at the sun burning down upon them. Then he glanced around at the buildings surrounding the monument as he did every year. So many new places had sprung up around it now. It was nothing like when it was first dedicated. It was so... modern now. There were still so many of the old places that he knew and loved, but now there were so many new places. And just so many more buildings.

He sighed quietly as he paused for a moment and inhaled the fresh, enjoyable, clean, salt air. He always loved being back in the Keys. They didn't live far away now, but they didn't come back here often enough for him. Not for this, but just to live and enjoy the beauty of the islands. But he knew that she could never 'forget' and enjoy it the way that he could. It was both of their homes, but she could never live here again.

Satisfied that the flowers had been arranged properly, his wife stepped back a few paces and looked at her work. Again satisfied with what she saw, she turned around and stepped all the way back to her husband now and gave him a warm embrace and a light kiss on his cheek. Pressing her face into his shoulder for a moment, she wiped away a tear, just like she did every year. Then, letting her hand fall to her side, Amy silently slipped her hand back into Jason's as they walked back to their car without saying another word.

A Brief Introduction to Henry Flagler and His Amazing Overseas Railroad

2:33 PM, January 22nd, 1912

The crowd's size continued to swell with the enormous number of people cramming their way onto the platform. Although to call it a platform was really a bit of hyperbole. The small wooden structure had been built hastily, and quite poorly for that matter, in the last few days to accommodate the large group of dignitaries who had been assembled for the auspicious occasion. Not only was the construction of the structure itself poor in design, but so was the estimation of the number of people that it would be required to hold. Given the length of time that they had had in order to build it, the general thought would have been that those in charge were just negligent in their duty. Such was not the case however. Instead, it seemed to lend even more value to the reason that they had all gathered here today on the rickety structure as it groaned and swayed back and forth beneath the overwhelming weight which threatened at any moment to overtake its structural integrity. No one seemed to give the impending doom any notice though, as the underwhelming platform itself only raised the people upon it a mere foot above the ground. It was more about the notoriety of being upon it, than anything else that gave the platform such importance. And the fact that no one of value had been around to create a structure of value was what lent so much importance to the impending event. Everyone who had any ability to build anything of value had had other plans in the last few years. The pair of delinquent drunks who had gotten the bid to build the platform, did not display in their craftsmanship the excitement and appreciation that they should have felt for finally having been able to gain some employment. But again, that was unfortunately due to the fact that they had no craftsmanship to display, which was why they had not previously secured any other bids.

Still, despite the poor construction and the blazing heat, the buzz that continued to grow upon the platform with every passing moment was both deafening and exhilarating at the same time. People were sweating in their Sunday best as they waved their hand-held fans rapidly back and forth in the humid heat that beat down on the predominantly, proud, smiling faces. No one remained in the city proper. The streets were empty and businesses were deserted. *Everyone* had turned out today.

He was coming today!

It was coming today!

Living in the Keys, the people were no strangers to the blazing heat of the sun, but even they were surprised by the unusual heat wave that was washing over the small, unassuming, little islands that dangled from the foot of the long, aptly named, sunshine state. And despite the fact that 1912 had been an unusually cold winter everywhere around the world, including within the US, that was definitely not the case today. Actually, it was so much the opposite of the cold weather that they had recently been experiencing in the low hanging islands, that they were now close to setting a record high for the month of January. In a way though, the unexpected and unexplainable near record heat wave in the middle of the coldest winter in memory made complete sense. Everything seemed crazy and unexplainable today. It was as if the world was about to be turned upside down. And for this little string of islands dangling down below at the bottom of the recently developed and increasingly populated Floridian peninsula, it was!

He was coming today!

It was coming today!

Oblivious for the most part to the reason for the excitement, or just simply not caring about it, a little boy sat on top of his father's shoulders smiling broadly as he licked at the ice cream cone and the vanilla ooze that ran continuously down his hand in small streams of sticky, white treasure. They were little drips that were turning into engorged raging rivers of melted ice cream. Doing little to thwart the melted ice cream's swift, methodical procession down his arm other than licking at it enthusiastically, the boy continued smiling unfazed by his lack of success at containment. His other hand continued to squeeze the string attached to the helium balloon floating above his head with a death like grip despite the fact that the end of the string was tied securely around his wrist. He had already been forewarned by his father that if he lost his balloon, that there would not be a new one to replace it. Despite his best efforts, periodically his grip would loosen as his attention drifted elsewhere to all of the amazing sights and scenes before him, but always the balloon stayed with him bobbing gently up and down above him in the warm, winter breeze.

The island's large population, or at least it certainly seemed large this morning, all appeared to be gathered together at this one spot, further crowding onto the seemingly outmatched, yet perpetually persevering platform. In excess of 10,000 people yelled, shouted, laughed, cheered and jostled one another to get a prime position for this astonishing, once-in-a-lifetime event. The dignitaries who were present had arrived from all over the United States and the world. Grand celebrations of every type had been planned for the next two weeks. Circus entertainers had come to the island to delight its inhabitants with their incredible and exotic talents. Everything had been made ready.

He was coming today!

It was coming today!

The little boy's father could not decide which was more impressive, the man or the machine, but the boy knew. He could not have been more than a day or two over six years old, but this boy was entirely certain that he was about to see the most amazing sight that he would ever experience in his whole lifetime.

The father was pretty certain as well though. He was certain that both were incredible. Prior to *Him*, Florida was a virtually unknown entity outside its borders. No one ever thought about the state, let alone ever considered visiting the lovely, yet lonely peninsula. People knew about the beauty of the Keys, but unless you already lived there, getting all the way down to them was near impossible for anyone less than the absolute wealthiest. But *He* was changing that!

Suddenly, the crowd seemed to grow even louder and more fevered than they had been only moments before. The machine was only 13 minutes past the time that it was due to arrive, but somehow the crowd seemed to sense that its arrival was drawing near. Just at that moment, they could hear distantly a voice rise above the rest of the din of the crowd. It came from the man who stood atop the apex of the beautiful new brick building that was the focal point of everyone's attention for the last 5 years as it was being built, and then later stocked with supplies, to bring out to the workers on the final leg of the project.

And interestingly enough, this was the majority of the work that the townspeople had actually seen on the railroad. A need to speed up the process had led to the workers beginning their efforts from Key West and moving out in order to make the whole process move faster as opposed to waiting for the tracks to be laid all the way from the mainland inward to the final key. *He* was getting older and he was anxious to see the completion of his dream. The crews had met a good distance out from Key West and had connected the two rails together at that distant point, but most of the locals living on the island never got to witness any of this work unless they were actually doing the work themselves or were willing to sneak out on boats to catch a glimpse.

The little boy strained to hear, pushing up with his legs against his father's body as he tried to get himself closer to the event. In all of the excitement, his ice cream cone was once more momentarily forgotten as he got caught up in the thrill of the moment. The ice cream ran down his arm now like a river that had finally broken free of its constricting dam, dripping harmlessly to the concrete below from the crook of his elbow; or at least the part that missed his father's shirt could have been considered harmless. Some of it also was smeared onto the people pressed up against the boy and his father in the crowd, but the people surrounding them also paid it no attention.

Sadly, so many years from now mother nature would burst through a handful of these tiny, little Key islands with as much ease as the ice cream that was now cascading down the young 10-year-old boy's hand today. But no one present there could possibly have known the impact that storm would one day have on John's life. The boy was very small for his age, very immature and he demonstrated none of the physical or mental attributes that would one day soon define who he was. Destined to grow up to be quite the local athlete, very mature and exceptionally good with the ladies, he displayed none of those characteristics yet.

The crowd had suddenly grown quieter as everyone strained to hear the man with the binoculars that stood high atop the brick building now pointing in the direction of the tracks that disappeared into the bright blue waters. "It's coming!" was all the man was able to get out before the swell of the crowd's voices once again drowned him out. The full military band snapped to attention and immediately kicked up the first of many tunes they had prepared in honor of the great happening. The small group of 25 to 30 young kids who had been standing around fidgeting as they waited impatiently for the action began dutifully yelling out the words to the first song they had memorized for the occasion.

It was still a few moments, before the massive machine began to slowly materialize from the beautiful nothingness that stretched out before them. The small roll of the waves from the clear, beautiful water below the tracks had a mesmerizing effect. But soon, God's glory was replaced by that of man's. *It* began to roll into view. The boy who was perched atop his father's shoulders stared in awe now. Everything else was forgotten and time seemed to slow to a crawl. First, the smoke that bellowed from the top of the stack became visible. The white smoke puffed out in a continuous stream disappearing into the blue skies above. The dark black body of the massive beast was next. The tracks shook and rattled as the great bellowing machine strained to pull itself nearer and nearer. The wheels squealed as the brakes were applied and the monstrous behemoth began to slow.

The train was still moving quickly, but its rate of approach had dropped drastically. It was coasting into the station right at 2:43 PM. Certainly not perfect timing, but for an undertaking that many people only a few years earlier had thought impossible, and most people thought was absurd, it was pretty damn impressive. In fact, it was amazingly impressive. Beyond words, impressive. It could have been an hour or two late arriving and it still would have been impressive. The accomplishment of even finishing the journey itself made everything else about the feat feel more than it was. Impressive was simply the only easy way to describe it.

Gliding majestically into full view, the little boy could now clearly see the giant, round snub nose of the engine as it pulled the three cars along behind it, slipping into the crowd of adoring citizens. In fact, the only thing holding the crush of the mob back from getting too close to the dangerous tracks, were the line of crisply dressed sailors who blocked the ordinary folks from making that kind of a foolish, life-threatening error in judgment. And although the sailors were dressed in their honorary uniforms, and were not there as a show of force, it made no difference. The respect that the crowd showed for the military men made actual, traditional crowd control measures pointless. Just the mere presence of the distinguished military men in their sharp-dressed uniforms with their arms crossed behind their backs, caused the crowd's decision-making process to do something foolish, highly unlikely.

The boy felt the sway of his father's body below him as he began to move forward. His father seemed to be as inexplicably drawn to the great display as everyone else around him. His forward momentum stopped quickly though. No one was able to move forward any further at this point. There simply was not enough room left for all of the thousands of people to squeeze any closer together. The platform was already full and well beyond what might have been its true capacity.

Then the crowd gasped and fell silent as the train settled home. The great beast had finally shuddered to a grinding halt and shifted backwards to its final resting spot after its long, amazing inaugural trip. The black of the metal was highly polished and shined brilliantly in the sun forcing many people in the crowd to put a hand up to block the painful rays from their eyes. One last thunderous exhalation by the great smoke pipe and all was momentarily quiet. The band had stopped, and most people had grown silent as if waiting for something wonderful and exciting to happen to put the exclamation point onto the whole event.

And then it did. *He* stepped forth! The door to railcar number 91 opened, and the man who otherwise might have been a god at that moment, slowly stepped forth and took in the moment with a sigh and a smile.

Henry Flagler had aged quite a bit by the time his now infamous train had made its first historic run, but the older man still had a spring left in his step. And it was especially evident on this day. The joy and relief that he felt from finally completing his life's work for the last twenty plus years added to that extra special hop that he had in his gait. As his now snow-white topped head appeared from within, the crowd went even crazier than they had been previously.

He stood on the edge of his car named *Rambler* teetering, assisted by the third Mrs. Flagler, Mary Lily, who being a great deal younger than he, was easily able to assist him. Despite the extra pep in his step that day, he was still an old man now, who had lived a long and full life. As he struggled to stare out through the glare of the blazing sun at the crowds that waited adoringly for him, his failing eyesight caused him to murmur with a mixture of grief and happiness, "I can hear the kids singing, but I cannot see them. They sound beautiful." Turning away from his wife to a friend who stood completely unnoticed behind the man, he whispered, "Now I can die happy. My dream is fulfilled."

Tears rolled openly down his jubilant face as he turned back to the people who now pressed forward, reaching out to touch the great machine, and some of them even being lucky enough to reach out and touch the man himself through the thin metal bars of railcar number 91 as he waved to the adoring crowds. American flags waved as far as the eyes could see, women wept openly, and men yelled out in uncontained joy. The man who had created the 8th wonder of the world, who had created a bridge across God's great creation of open expansive water, who had tamed the wild wetlands of the harsh Floridian peninsula, who had spent more than a fortune chasing a fools dream, and who had traveled over 128 miles of marsh, land and water until finally at long last, he had arrived!

35 Years Earlier - The Floridian Experiment Begins

Mid-afternoon, Monday, October 15th, 1877

The 47-year-old tycoon sat in his large, plush chair looking at his favorite painting, which stood high on the mantle well above his fireplace. He pondered the beauty of the work, as he often did, while he sat reflecting on his days' work and what needed to be done tomorrow. He had come a long way since his failed days of owning the Flagler and York Salt Company. Sure, he and his brother-in-law had done well enough in the early days with the business while the War of Southern Aggression had been transpiring. But once President Lincoln had crushed the rebellion and ended the hated civil war, there was no longer a great need for their expensive, wonderful preservative mineral. Those early days of enormous debt had been tough on him. He thought about the early days with John Rockefeller, and his other partner Samuel Andrews, who had helped Henry secure the money to start the business.

Looking back on where they had been and the struggles that they had survived made him appreciate even more where they were at now. What a rousing success Standard Oil had become. Never would Henry have to worry about money again. His friend John was an incredible businessman. They had literally gone from nothing, to the largest oil refinery in the states, within two years. Henry still shook his head in bewilderment and amazement any time he stopped to think about it. He had always known that Rockefeller had a nose for this sort of thing, but still this kind of unbelievable growth had always seemed beyond the realm of possibility. Quite frankly it amazed him to think about what John had done with that initial investment of $100,000. Their partnership just seemed to have a flow about it. Henry felt like they had a better working relationship than anyone he had ever met before. Every idea that they thought of, they worked and created together. Never had two minds worked in unison so well.

"Henry." John Rockefeller's voice cut through his thoughts and dragged him back to the present.

"John." Henry Flagler stood up to meet his friend and partner as he walked into the room.

The taciturn Henry shook hands firmly with his more extravagant, flamboyant partner. Henry motioned for the younger man to sit.

"Good to see you again my friend. How is it I get to town and you are leaving me already?" John joked with his older friend, a smile on his lips as he gave the slight jab.

"If your ridiculous 'look-at-me-I-am-the-greatest-man-in-the-world' ego didn't get in your way, you would have been here spending time with the people who *really* care about you!" Henry dead-paned his own good-natured jab back at his friend. John Rockefeller was well known for his lavish lifestyle and his grandiose nature of charitable giving. "Off to save some orphaned children somewhere, are you?"

"ME?" John asked in mock incredulity. "I am not the one who is preparing to go to the jungles of the Confederate traitors."

"Hmm, yes. I remember how valiantly you paid to *not* go fight the evil southerners yourself."

"Hey." John's feigned anger almost seemed convincing this time. Henry always wondered if those jabs about John's lack of involvement in the war actually hit home or not. "That cost me a fair amount of money to help defeat those devilish folks. They threatened to ruin my economic endeavors. And yours as well, I might point out. In fact, you should be thanking me profusely for helping to destroy their fiendish plots."

"Yes. More stoking of the ego for the 'great one'!"

"So, tell me..." John's demeanor turned serious as he ignored his friend's latest genial jab and instead addressed the real issue that Henry knew he was here to discuss. "Are you really heading down there for good?"

"John," Henry was already exasperated by the conversation that they had previously held so many times before. "I told you, the doctor has told me... No! Instructed me in fact, that it is the best thing for her. I have no choice. We'll be fine..." Henry waived his hand dismissively.

"Fine? Fine?!? Do you know what they have down there?" He waited just a breath for dramatic effect, slapping the armrest of his chair for added emphasis. "Nothing! There is nothing down there for you. You are going to Jackson Village, right? What do they have down there, 5,000 persons. 6,000?!? Do they even own a theatre? Where will you eat? How will you live?"

"Posh." Henry waved his hands in the air at his friend. "You make it sound as if they are all Indian savages down there without an ounce of sophistication among them."

"And am I wrong about that?"

"John, please. Jackson-*ville*." He emphasized the end of the city's name for good measure. "Which you know full well is the name of the city. And yes, it has plenty of culture. Plus, they also have Key West as well."

"Key West?!? Key West?!? Do not play me the fool Henry. How will you get to Key West? Will you swim? Will you take the steamer to Key West? Maybe jump on a military supply boat? Please," John almost spit the word from his mouth. "Key West... Just tell me that you will not catch some exotic disease down there and bring it back to the rest of us sane folk."

John stood up and marched around the room, restlessly, unsuccessfully, trying to wrestle with the idea of his best friend moving to a land of scrub brush and swamps. He stopped for a second and looked back at Henry earnestly. "Stay here and help me with Standard." His words were almost pleading in their tone.

Henry stood up and gripped his friend by his shoulders, a slight scowl that typically passed for a smile gripped Henry's face as he addressed his long-time friend, "Who knows John. Maybe one day you will come down to visit me."

"Please..." John moved towards the door firmly, but not irritably, breaking his friend's grasp, "do not threaten me so, my friend. I may have to find a new best friend even sooner than I had anticipated."

Henry moved with his friend to the foyer. "I promise I will be safe." As they stopped in front of the door, he looked his friend squarely in the eye, he solemnly promised him again. "I will return shortly. I have no desire to remain down there any longer than the weather will require of us. I shall be back in a few short months and we'll attack! Standard will be stronger than ever."

John turned to the door, grabbed the handle and stopped just before leaving. "You better honor your promise Henry. I have no desire to go down there to exact my revenge on you if you don't."

Henry grimaced once more at his friend's back as he slipped away and out the door. Florida... He wondered one more time if his good friend didn't have it right. What the hell was he thinking!

Unfortunately for Henry, it would not be for another 35 years that he would find out that he was indeed doing the right thing.

And perhaps fittingly, he would not be alive another 23 years after that when his greatest creation would also die.

8:06 AM, Friday, August 30th, 1935

3 days until the hurricane

Storm clouds rolled in the distance as the sky began to darken over the waters of the Straits of Florida. To the East, if you had been able to see far enough, the storm would have looked much like any other. But no one could see that far. Not even the new "weather machines," as they called them, that were reportedly being used throughout the country now with great fanfare and expectation. There was no hint of the destruction that was only 3 days away from Islamorada.

The first weather reports of a new storm beginning to develop far off the east coast of Florida began to trickle in slowly. But no one took them seriously. No reports were issued to the general public. Twenty-three years after the Eighth Wonder of the World had been completed and ordained as such, the islanders of this tropical paradise would never stand a chance against the true number one wonder of this world, Mother Nature.

8:08 AM, Friday, August 30th, 1935

3 days until the hurricane

Jason opened the large, heavy door to the long, crowded hall and grudgingly slipped inside. The school was small, as everything on the beautiful, little, tranquil island of Key West was. The whole island was only 4 miles long by 1 mile wide. And even though the population was as big as, or bigger than, any other city in Florida, most of the time it didn't feel that way. It just all felt "small." Besides, even being the largest city in Florida, didn't actually mean that you were big. It just meant that you were the largest fish in their tiny little pond.

People passed him by swiftly, moving quickly in both directions. The second bell had already been rung by the administrator standing at the far end with the large brass bell in hand and most of the kids were moving rapidly now with a purpose. A few of them didn't truly care if they were late to class or not, but still they had other places that they did want to go. Whatever their purpose, they were all moving, even the ones who didn't look like they cared to move were shuffling along now. And Jason was no different. He stared straight ahead with the same unfocused, unhappy gaze that graced the face of almost every typical high school teenager at some time or another since the beginning of time as he sauntered slowly down the discolored marble floor.

Every type of person existed within these high school halls. Starting at the top of the hierarchy, the athletes and cool kids, who all reflexively looked away if he dared to make eye contact with them swiftly passed him by. The newly formed club of cheer leaders also fell into that category and was made up of only the most important people it seemed. They too could not bear to look at someone like him for too long. Some of these popular kids however, didn't even have the common courtesy to look away fast enough so that he would not have to endure the look of disdain or utter annoyance that appeared as spasms across their beautiful faces. It was as if they were shocked that he was even willing to show up at "their" school and cause them the discomfort of having to be in the same vicinity as him.

A small percentage of the cool kids fell into that rare high school breed who knew they were cool, but still understood that they weren't "better" than the rest of them. They could stand to be around the lower-class people such as Jason. They usually chose not to, because, well... Honestly, if Jason could have hung around the cool kids all the time, would he really have hung around with kids like himself? He would have loved to have answered yes, but if he was being honest with himself, probably not. In the end, the cool kids were, well... cool!

He walked past the kids who were middling at best. They weren't considered good enough to be "cool", but they certainly were not going to risk their perilous position in the delicate high school hierarchy to make actual eye contact with Jason for anything more than a few seconds. Maybe a head nod or a half-smile, but nothing significant that might draw attention to themselves.

The funny twist to being a "middling" was that the other middling student was staring back at you thinking the same thing. Two normal teenagers passing each other in the hall, each one struggling inwardly, trying to figure out who was cooler and who had the upper hand. Who should be nodding to whom, and who should be looking away as the inferior. In the strange, and often times debilitating, world of the teenage hierarchy, not many kids in that level ever considered the fact that neither should have to avert their gaze. It simply had become a given that someone had to be the dominant, more important class. And failing that realization, it usually meant that both of them were so far outside the realm of the high school royalty that they just no longer cared or no longer had a shot at being anything other than what they already were.

As it turns out, many years later when he had grown up, Jason would find that he did not see it as much different when he left school and entered the real world. Adults just seemed to hide the reality of their hierarchal constraints better than the students.

He saw the misfits. The kids that no one would speak to, not even Jason. As a lower level middling at best himself, he nodded politely to some of the misfit faces he saw. Some of them nodded back to him, some of them gave him the same scornful looks that he had received from the cool kids. Their purpose for scowling was anger and rejection. They had already had enough of trying to fit in to the unforgiving, complex world of the teenage chain of command. They had tried and failed too many times. They didn't have the skills, the want, the blessings of good looks, the money or whatever other distinction or merit was needed to rise above their current status. They had either given up on high school and were already looking ahead to a new start at another level, be it college or the real world, or they had just simply given up altogether.

And quite literally, for the majority of them, college was never even an option. Those who could afford college, and were smart enough, did not have many choices.

A new university close to them, the University of Miami, had just been founded in 1925, but in reality, it might have been an entire world away from Key West. And with a small student body population, the university had almost folded entirely during the last few years, even being reduced to having had to file for bankruptcy a couple of years back.

Then there was the University of Florida founded earlier in 1906 which had thousands of students now, but there was almost no chance of ever getting there as it was even further away than the University of Miami in the northern part of the state in a sleepy, little town called Gainesville.

True, they were now connected to the mainland of Florida thanks to the foolhardy Henry Flagler and his magnificent Overseas Railroad, but yet even today the connection to the mainland remained tenuous at best for most of the Key's inhabitants. They just didn't have the means for such long-range travel. The Dixie Highway that Carl Fisher promoted and spearheaded in 1914 connected the Southern US from the bottom of Florida all the way up to Canada in the same way that his "cross-country" highway had done the year before in connecting Washington DC to San Francisco. Even that, however, still didn't make it practical. Very few people in the Keys had the kind of money necessary to make trips like that. And the population of the Keys at this time was not made up of poor families! But the great depression was "great" for a reason; it had affected everyone, big and small.

Whatever the reason, Jason didn't much care, just the same as any other day; he had his own battles to fight over with "fitting in". He couldn't slow down to worry about anyone else's trials and tribulations. Putting his head down, he shouldered his sack of school supplies higher onto his back and pushed through the heavy wooden door into his first class of the day. As the noise, anarchy and heat of the packed room beyond burst over his body like a tidal wave, he sighed. It was time to give it his all. He certainly was not referring to his class work though. He simply had to grind out his day without any missteps. Make sure he didn't say anything that could be mistaken as stupid or worth making fun of. Try to get in one or two funny comments with some kids above his status without ever actually engaging them in the dangerous perils of prolonged conversation. These quick hits, as he mentally referred to them, allowed him to be seen and heard in a good light without him having to hold an extended conversation where he may accidentally make a gaffe or say something stupid. It was a cowardly way to live, but it was the best he could ever get himself to rise to.

Sadly, being so engrossed in his own inner hand wringing, he never even noticed the attractive girl who watched him push his way into his classroom. Amy had momentarily smiled wryly at his back before she had shuffled off to disappear into her own classroom. One day, she thought.

Jason meanwhile, oblivious to her thoughts and wistful stare, looked up with dread at the large wooden clock that hung high upon the wall as he shoved himself the rest of the way into the room. 8:10 AM. The clock was now ticking. He now had roughly 7 hours to complete his mission, surviving another Friday at school. It never seemed like a sure bet that he would succeed, but then again, he didn't have any other options.

1:13 PM, Friday, August 30th, 1935

3 days until the hurricane

"Mom. Mom..." The sweet little girl with the Shirley Temple curls, so recently made famous by the now newly famous child actor, pulled on her mother's dress. "MOMMY!"

"What, young lady? Mommy is speaking. What could possibly be so important?" The attractive, smartly dressed woman, who appeared to be dressed for a Sunday morning church service peered patiently, yet clearly exasperated down at her darling, little girl.

"When is the train going to leave?" Her daughter looked up at her sweetly with such innocence that she could have given Ms. Temple herself a run for her money.

"Ahh." Her mother rolled her eyes and turned back to her girlfriend who was accompanying them on their exciting Labor Day Weekend trip. "I've told you a thousand times already, Patty." She glanced back down at her daughter who had already turned away from her as well and was bouncing excitingly on the railing again, "The train should..."

Her mother's voice was cut short by the loud whistle of the huge machine that stood waiting patiently in front of them being tended to busily by the workers who scampered around making it ready for their latest passengers. "The train is now ready for boarding at your convenience ladies and gentlemen. Please watch your step as you enter the train. And enjoy your travels on the legendary Eighth Wonder of the World!"

The porters continued running around, grabbing bags to load onboard, and directing families, students and other expectant vacationers to their proper seats and cars.

"Ah, see." The relief was palpably evident in the society woman's voice. "Here we go, my dear." Being over an hour late boarding the train with a five-year-old who was already wired from not having to go to school and experiencing her first trip on the wondrous Overseas Railroad was enough to fray anyone's nerves.

"I still don't understand the 'Flagler's Folly' moniker," her friend began again, getting back to their previous conversation that had been interrupted by Sharon's daughter. "So, at first no one thought that it could be built? Then, he does build it, proving everyone wrong. Everyone's amazed and it gets international acclaim for being the Eighth Wonder of the World. And now, everyone's back to saying that it's a disaster and they're mocking the guy again. The poor man's not even around to defend himself any longer." Tina made the sign of the cross as she looked quickly up to the skies above and blew them a kiss. "It doesn't make sense. And," she added quickly, "it doesn't seem fair either."

"Well Tina," Sharon put on her most serious, I'm-educated-and-know-these-things-and-you-don't voice, "the train has lost lots of money. They say that the government wants to close it because it costs so much money. I couldn't tell you how much, of course, but there are rumors..." Sharon paused dramatically and looked around as if someone might be listening. "There are rumors that they may have even lost more than $10 million dollars."

Tina gasped at the unthinkable amount of money. "Well, I heard that however much money they lost, it was all from Mr. Flagler's *personal accounts*. Can you imagine?"

The two young ladies continued chatting as they moved aboard the train and made their way to their seats. Settling in as they continued debating the magnitude of 'Mr. Flagler's great loss', they prepared themselves for the ride of their lives.

2 PM, Friday, August 30th, 1935

3 days until the hurricane

"Hey Gramps, ya goin' into town today? Tony checked with the big boss. It's true! They're offering free passage to all workers this weekend, to and from Key West. I done got my ticket already. I have a little beer money saved up that I intend to invest into the economy for good ol' Uncle Sam."

The grizzled old man who went by Gramps, and whose real name wasn't even known by any of the men that he now shared the construction site with, threw a look to his younger companion which read, "Why the hell are you even bothering to ask me?" But just to be sure, Gramps followed up his look with an actual audible reply that said exactly that, but with a bit more "color" to it.

"Well personally, I think ya'll is nuts. With the way this government's fallin' apart, this might be the last chance that a couple of old grunts like you and me get to go party for quite some time. Hell, if they weren't offering free passage, courtesy of Old-Mr.-Money-Bags-Himself, Henry Flagler, God rest his soul, then I wouldn't be able to afford no beer, no how to begin with. So come on, Gramps. What d'ya say? Wanna hop on over to party with the Conchs tonight with me?" Not even bothering to wait for the salty soldier's response, and not expecting to get a decent one anyhow, the younger soldier pressed on. "Well, if you ain't gonna join us, and you got nothin' else to offer, how 'bout ya at least throw me one of those extra Luckies you got? I could really do with a smoke to git through this last hour or so 'fore the train gits on in here."

The old soldier continued to lean with arms crossed on top of the wooden end of his shovel for a moment enjoying the break from his work. Squinting with one eye he turned to stare up at the other young man who stood just a bit off to one side mimicking him by resting in a similar stance on his own shovel. "Sounds like our pesky friend here lost all of his Lucky Strikes at poker last night, don't you think Hawkeye?"

Greg Shaver's nickname came from his impressive marksmanship as a sniper for the US infantry. A terror during the Great War with his standard sniper issue US M1903 Springfield Rifle, at 37 years of age he still looked capable of fighting off an army full of Germans. Snipers were a new breed in the war, and that's exactly what Greg was in war, a new, very dangerous breed. But back in civilian life, he liked just being Greg. Around the guys though, he couldn't escape the deadly moniker. No matter how genial he was, they knew who he "truly" was. Greg just gave a slight grin and shrugged.

Gramps made a short sound that for other people might have come out as a chuckle, but instead for him came out as a gruff indescribable sound that seemed to imply some type of enjoyment. "One." Gramps pulled out of his shirt pocket and held up a single cigarette but held back throwing it to his fellow compatriot. "But..." he waved the cigarette around enticingly, "you owe me *three* when you get your next pack." Gramps smiled warmly now, showing off both of his teeth.

Johnny's smile turned to a scowl, "Ya son-of-a-bitch. You know I can't say no to that. I need one. Come on! You can't do this to me." Gramps face didn't change one bit. "Fine. Not much of a friend, is ya?" Johnny grumbled for another minute or two before his face broke into a smile as he casually let his shovel fall to the ground and he shuffled over to accept his newly bargained-for prize. "Ah, what the hell. I'm fixin' to have a good ol' time in Key West. This is gonna be a great weekend. What could possibly go wrong with me roaming around free in Key West?" He popped his cig into his mouth and then jammed both thumbs into his shirt as his new, unlit prize dangled precariously from his pursed lips with a big goofy smile all over his beaming face.

Then, just as quickly, Johnny let the unlit cigarette drop to dangle loosely from his now open mouth and looked up suddenly with a crushed look upon his face. No more than half a moment after the cigarette touched his lips, the first large rain drop had landed on the top of his head. "Aw, great," he mumbled.

4 PM, Friday, August 30th, 1935

3 days until the hurricane

The train glided along as if on a bed of air. Looking out the window, the little girl was amazed to see that the land had fallen away as they lifted off from the mainland. She had never flown like a bird of course, but this was most definitely what she had always imagined it would be like. Her head stuck out through the small window, she could feel the wind whipping through her hair, threatening to pull her right off the seat where she stood on her tip-toes. Her mother's firm grip on her tiny waist made certain that nothing like that would happen naturally, but still the restricting feel of her mother's arm did little to steal away the feeling of total freedom.

Most of the time as she looked down, there was nothing below, just beautiful, pristine blue waters that practically begged little Patty to dive right in. She continued wiggling and pulling at her mother's grip as she tried to get closer and closer.

Her mother meanwhile sat chatting away with her friend of many years. Tina had been with her family since the time when they were children. She was not a servant or anything. They had simply grown up together and had never really parted. Despite the fact that Sharon had been sent away for school to be properly trained for a number of years, the distance between them did nothing to split the friendship and bonds that the two women had developed in childhood and always continued to share. Even the very wide discrepancy in family wealth and status did little to cause friction between the two naturally, inseparable women. True they had their squabbles every now and then, just as all friends do from time to time, but for the most part, they were thick as thieves.

And as the modern miracle of man continued to glide along, every now and then, even the older, more experienced women, had to look out over the edge and ooh at the sights which their eyes beheld. They were truly awe-inspiring vistas of God's creation.

As the train continued on its four-hour trek from the young bustling city of Miami, it would make numerous stops along the way. Little towns dotted the small "key" islands once they had left the mainland behind. It made the trains time from Miami to Key West a great deal longer than it could have been, but most of the riders did not mind the extra time on board. For many of them, this was truly a 'ride of a lifetime'. The luxuriousness of the train, even in the general population cars, was way above what the typical Floridians of the time were normally exposed to or even able to afford. And, for the most part the weather complied extremely well. There was very little indication of the storm that was moving ever closer to the areas that they were crossing over at those very moments.

4:39 PM, Friday, August 30th, 1935

3 days until the hurricane

US Army Veteran Camp on Matecumbe Key

"Well what do you suppose this might be?" Tina asked as they strained their necks to see out of the opposite side windows as the train slowed for yet another stop.

"I'll bet this is a camp for those poor soldiers. You know the ones that marched up to Washington only to get pushed out by that bully from the army, Mr. MacArthur." Tina practically bit at the civilian title for the career army man. Her disdain written all over her face and dripping from her voice. She, like most of the population at the time who were familiar with the now infamous event, was on the side of the marchers, not that of Washington.

"I heard that General MacArthur had to do it in order to maintain order..." Tina started timidly, using the army chief of staff's proper title.

In matters of politics, Tina had always deferred to her "smarter," "better bred," and "more educated" friend, which was just the way Sharon preferred it. And this instance was no different. Sharon swatted away her attempt at input without a thought. "Oh, be quiet now Tina." Sharon dismissed her as if she were speaking to a child, a belief which in Sharon's mind was not too far from the truth with regards to Tina's mental acumen. "That's simply not true. He easily could..." Sharon immediately dropped her previous train of thought at the sight of a nearby porter. "Ah, sir. Sir...?" Her imperious, demanding voice grated upon the porter's nerves from the first syllable that she uttered, causing him to continue moving along on his initial path without hesitation, putting him at risk of more of her ire. "Can you tell me what manner of station this is?"

The porter never turned to acknowledge her, having already heard some of the previous discussion. "Yes ma'am. You are correct. These are the brave souls of the Bonus Marchers." He seemed to have quite a bit of reverence in his voice as he made the statement, stooping a bit to be able to see out the same window that the two ladies had been trying to see through earlier.

Sharon, miffed at how she was so easily dismissed and ignored, snorted her derision, changing her entire demeanor regarding the poor lot beyond. "Looks like a dirty, rabble of people, if you ask me."

Actually, the society woman was not in fact able to make out any of the infamous Bonus Marchers. Not only because her field of vision would not have permitted it from her angle at that moment, but also because many of them had either already packed for the free passage they had been allotted for this special weekend trip and were busily boarding the train further down the line or because they had already retired for the day back to their makeshift homes. Even the workers who were not going on the trip were released early that day in order to celebrate the long weekend.

Those workers who were taking advantage of the trip had been assigned their own particular area of the train that had been reserved entirely for them. And in fact, the area was not any worse than that which was occupied by the higher brow passengers either. The railroad had been instructed to take "the very best care of our country's backbone". And that was exactly what they were doing.

Having already mentally dismissed the porter, she completely missed the short and barely concealed look of withering disdain that he threw over his shoulder in her direction. Being only a porter, he certainly could not afford the chance of offending one of the society passengers. His whole life depended on keeping this job. It was the only thing he knew. One ill word from her to the wrong person and he would never work for the company again. Or any railroad company for that matter!

Still, her attitude made him sick. These men had been willing to sacrifice everything for her freedom and she treated them as though they were common street urchins. And *Mr.* Douglas MacArthur as she derisively referred to him, was the army's youngest major general ever and chief of staff for the entire United States Army. As far as the porter was concerned, slighting either party was equally reprehensible. With one last withering glance, he quietly slid out the door in front of them and fervently hoped to himself that he would never have to look upon her visage again.

Tina took note of the porter's scathing look back at Sharon but felt absolutely no compulsion to point it out to her companion. Sharon had already forgotten he existed. What she did notice however, was what had appeared outside of the now wide-open door. Although Sharon and Tina never did see any of the men themselves, they certainly could see the small makeshift town that had been hastily put together for them at the order of President Franklin D. Roosevelt. President Roosevelt had shipped many of the Bonus Marchers off to camps in the south. Among them was this camp at Matecumbe Key, its sister camp also on Matecumbe Key and another at Windley Key.

Tina was the first to speak. "Look at the camp!" Tina could not keep the sound of shock and horror out of her voice. "People should not have to live like that." She paused for a moment in horror, her eyes continuing to scan the makeshift tents. "They look like homes for animals."

The train was significantly elevated above the flat, even land of the long, thin Key. One of the first Keys to be reached when leaving the mainland, the train was still well above the makeshift camp as it stopped at the ragged excuse for a station. What had met the train when it had finally shuddered to a complete stop was little more than a shaky wooden platform. Beyond the "station" area was spread out a vast number of tent tops. Sharon and Tina would later both swear up and down that they had seen well over fifty or sixty of the ragged looking temporary homes, although in reality there were in fact no more than thirty in the immediate vicinity. And of these, they could only make out a handful of tents at the most. The other tents had been established much further away from the rail and could never have been seen by the two traveling tourists.

Despite the slightly muted number of tents that greeted the young ladies attention, the shock of their dilapidated features was no less impactful.

It truly was a sorry sight to behold. It was obvious that at one point, the tents had been of excellent army construction, built to withstand some of the world's harshest environments and the most brutal of conditions. Today, however, they were far beyond their shelf life. Many of them appeared frayed and tattered. Some of them had outright holes that caused the wind to whistle as it whipped through their gloomy, porous surfaces. Tina and Sharon could only imagine the misery that must have been experienced during the rainy times, such as what they were currently enduring. Both women's faces, now Sharon's as well since the sting of the porter's comments had already receded, reflected the sickened visages of compassionate individuals looking upon a scene that no human being should be forced to bear.

And to make the situation more sickening, both women were very familiar with why the soldiers were there. The story of how the Bonus Army had been treated had been well documented by the press corps. The stories had spread quickly, even all the way down to the farthest corners of the country, such as in their little corner of the world in Miami.

There had been pictures in the newspapers of the soldiers camped in their dirty makeshift tents on the lawn of the white house, begging for help. It had been over three years now since the soldiers had made their way to Washington, D. C. in a spontaneous march for financial aid and assistance. Most of them had been unemployed and desperate. 20,000 veterans had camped in vacant government buildings, bent on making their voices heard and their plight recognized. For a while, they were orderly and peaceful. They were even made welcome by the police superintendent of the city, Pelham Glassford, according to the papers.

But then on June 17th, everything seemed to go terribly wrong.

The Patman Bill, named after Representative Wright Patman who had sponsored it, that had been seeking immediate payment of the soldier's bonus payments from the Great War, was defeated. But the more significant blemish on America's history was not until just over a month later. Already, it was being viewed as an affair that would go down in the young country's history books as something that no one would ever want remembered. But it was about to get worse. Significantly worse.

Tina began timidly again, continuing to use MacArthur's proper military title. "You started to say something about what General MacArthur could have done..."

"Ah yes. Sorry." Sharon broke free from her disheartened trance and added her teacher voice back into her inflection. "So, as I was saying, Mr. MacArthur could have easily handled it much better than the manner in which he did. Look at this rag-tag group." Sharon's arm swept out grandly in the direction of the debilitated camp ground, as if she was displaying some fancy new gadget for sale. "Are you telling me that the *Great* Mr. MacArthur could not have handled this group without bloodshed?" Her voice dripped with sarcasm when referring to both the Great MacArthur, whose military moniker she continued to intentionally refrain from using, and the ragtag Bonus Marchers. "Please!" She exaggerated the word, drawing it out for additional scorn and emphasis.

"And," she continued her lecture as if she had just remembered something vital to add, "what about the man who saved MacArthur's life?" Tina was almost certain that this was not something that had 'just been remembered' by Sharon. Her friend had quite the flare for the dramatic. "That poor man was *viciously and summarily mistreated and dismissed by the Great MacArthur!*"

Tina nodded dutifully as her friend wagged her finger accusatorily in her face, almost daring Tina to dispute any of the important wisdom that was being imparted upon her.

Sharon, momentarily distracted by her daughter, looked down to attend to her. Meanwhile, Tina rolled her eyes when she knew her friend was significantly distracted. She certainly did not feel like she was any less intelligent than her friend. And yet, she could kick herself right now for being so stupid. Tina most certainly knew better than to get Sharon started on a political or historical soliloquy when she was trapped with no avenue of escape for a long stretch of time like this. And yet here she was.

As Sharon looked back up from attending to her daughter, she struggled for a moment to remember where they had left off. Tina's hopes were raised for a moment and she sat up a little straighter in anticipation of a more enjoyable conversation as she saw Sharon's eyes look off into the distance for a minute as she struggled to reorient herself. Perhaps it was her lucky day and the conversation could be turned to a less exhausting topic. But that kind of luck was just not in the cards for her today.

"Oh yes, Mr. MacArthur…" Sharon began again. Tina's hopes dashed, her shoulders slouched back down as the train began pulling away from the Marchers camp and she prepared for a ride that suddenly seemed much less exhilarating.

4:39 PM, Friday, August 30th, 1935

3 days until the hurricane

Johnny shuffled his way back through the gently rocking train loaded full of soldiers, his hands grasping lightly onto each seat back for stability as he moved along, shaking his head in disbelief as he plopped down into his seat, still bewildered by their current accommodations. They were traveling in style on one of the greatest technological inventions the world had ever seen, and they were headed to a tropical island where the beer was cold, and the women were beautiful. He looked around at the small, handful of grizzled old soldiers who had joined him on the weekend voyage. Well, the beautiful women would be wasted on this group, he thought ruefully, but at least the cold beer wouldn't be. What a pitiful looking group.

And they were truly just that, a bunch of wretched, old soldiers. Johnny included. He certainly was not removing himself from that description. What a lousy lot we are, Johnny thought, as he glanced around at the weary faces that stared back at him. Just a bunch of misfit grunts who had no place else to be. None of us have two nickels to rub together, none of us have any women or kids to worry over us or care about us if we don't come home tonight, no responsibilities to think about. In a way it was reassuring, but in an even bigger way, it was extremely disheartening and gloomy at the same time. No one depends on us, yet there's no one there for us to be a part of either. We have each other and that's it. Now he really was depressed. He had no problem sharing a fox hole with any one of these guys, all of them were battle tested and tougher than nails. But... Being lifetime friends with these people? Most of these people were every bit as rotten as he was.

Just look at how we're dressed, he reflected gloomily. Barely enough time to even get a decent shower and change.

Johnny's life had been anything but the American dream. Oh sure, his family started poor, just like in the American dream. The only problem was, that seemed to be where they were going to end up as well. And if his family wasn't going to end up poor, Johnny was pretty darn certain that he was not going to be the one to raise the bar for them.

Who knew? Maybe he would eventually find a woman and have a kid. Maybe it would be his son or daughter who would raise the family name from less than dirt to something more prestigious. Johnny often daydreamed about being more than he actually was, but he always knew it was just that, a dream. Ambition was not Johnny's strongest suit. His mouth was. He could talk about anything for the most part. Not always intelligently, but he could definitely talk about it. For hours, in fact, if he felt like it. And most of the time he did. The great majority of the guys seemed pretty tolerant of him overall, although a few of them without a doubt took exception to how much he blabbered on about stuff.

It wasn't his fault though. He had a restless mind. Things just tended to pour out of his mouth. It was difficult for him to control at times. He just really liked telling people his thoughts. Even when he knew people didn't want to hear them. In fact, and he had trouble understanding why this was so, he seemed to particularly enjoy speaking his mind when he knew that they *didn't* want to hear his opinion.

As if he just realized that he hadn't spoken in over a minute or so, he looked around frantically for someone to talk to. The nearest men all knew to keep their heads down and not make eye contact with Johnny. Unfortunately for the new guy two seats over across the aisle, he was not aware of the impending danger.

"Hey new guy..." Johnny slid over a bit as the soldier across the way lifted his head to acknowledge that Johnny was speaking with him. "You know much about Key West?" The new guy looked left and right to be certain that this guy was actually addressing him and not someone else. Johnny leaned in further with great anticipation as he registered the soldier's response when he finally shrugged his shoulders and shook his head no. All the other soldiers around them smiled inwardly as Johnny stood up, moved over a few feet and plopped down next to him in an open seat. "Of course I've never been there myself either, but..." Now everyone knew as Johnny launched into his latest yarn that it would be a nice, peaceful ride into Key West. Well, at least for most of them anyhow...

6:15 PM, Friday, August 30th, 1935

3 days until the hurricane

Jason walked along beside the fence marveling at the changes in the people that passed by him. And yet none of them appeared to be truly any different than they were at school. They were still the same people that he had survived another week of school with, and yet, here at the football game they looked so different. Some of them looked so much happier, and some of them looked no happier. Some of them even looked that much worse, which hardly even seemed possible. But they all still had their hierarchical status written all over their stature and bearing. His mind briefly wandered to the fact that it was the "best of times, it was the worst of times". He shook his head and scowled angrily at himself. And he wondered why he didn't have friends. Even his thoughts were geeky.

He smiled politely at a couple of people, nodded in what he hoped appeared to be a cool, detached manner at a few others and made certain not to make eye contact with *many* others. It wasn't that he was afraid of them in the traditional sense. It was just that if he didn't look directly at them, he wouldn't have to worry about *how* to act. He felt like he could pull it off with the others, but the ones that he was avoiding, pretending like he didn't even notice, those were the cool kids; those were the ones where every look mattered. The wrong smile, the over eager hand wave, looking away too quickly or staring too long. There were so many traps lurking that he didn't even want to think about it, let alone contemplate making the effort to attempt tackling them by actually speaking to people.

No! Blending in and avoiding were the most reasonable means of averting disaster.

He stopped at the end of the fence and the beginning of the stands and looked up into the mass of humanity that rose up before him like a wall of insurmountable odds. He knew his parents would be up at the top, in their "usual" spot. He was pretty certain that they had not moved since high school. And yes, there they were again, just like every Friday night during football and baseball season, "holding court" as Jason liked to think of it. Doing everything *but* blending in!

His father was easily visible almost immediately. All Jason had to do was look for the center of attention. All around his father, friends and acquaintances sat mesmerized, staring at his three-ring circus as he gestured wildly. Surely, he was regaling them with some amazing exploit from his days of dominating on the grid iron for Jason's school. Even 17 years later, Jason was still known as "John's kid." The fact that Jason was obviously *not* "John's kid" didn't seem to vex anyone. Oh sure, John was definitely his biological father, he had just forgotten to pass along any athletic ability or social skills to his son.

Jason never really could understand how it was possible that they could be so different. And although to the outside world it might not seem like it at times, Jason worshiped the ground his father walked upon. All he wanted was to have $1/10^{th}$ of his father's athletic prowess..., or his wit..., or his way with the ladies... or pretty much any of the other traits that allowed him to mesmerize people whenever he felt like it, as it appeared he was doing effortlessly right now.

The crowd around John laughed loudly as his father came to what Jason had to assume was the culmination of another great yarn his father was spinning. The end of the story and the reaction of the crowd broke Jason free from his trance. Jason felt like these "trances" of his were getting more and more frequent and less and less "every now and then." And ironically enough, just as he was thinking about that, he turned to look out onto the field and immediately fell into another very deep trance. He couldn't take his eyes off of her. She was every male teenagers dream come true, and the envy of every one of the girls. She wasn't the captain of the new cheerleading squad, but Jason fervently believed that was only because she didn't want to be. In fact, this was the first year that they had a captain, one for the girls and one for the guys. It was a very controversial decision, but one they decided was necessary. The pep club had only started the year before that. At this time, they were very cutting edge even to have a club and *that* had been a very controversial decision. Most cheerleader clubs at this time were restricted to the prestigious colleges and were for the men only. Their club had 4 girls and 6 guys. The guys were much better at yelling since they were so much louder, but the girls certainly brought a lot of excitement to the club, along with a lot of anxious looks from the parents who were not so certain about this new development.

Their roles were very limited. They didn't move much, it was mostly arm movements, clapping and yelling. The long straight skirt that she wore fell almost completely to the ground. Every now and then as she swayed back and forth the tips of her shoes would peak out from below the heavy wool skirt. Her shy, yet somehow also confident smile seemed to brighten the entire world for Jason. He just knew that she was smiling only for him. It was strange that she could appear so demure and shy, yet at the same time, he knew she had unbelievable amounts of courage.

She could have been anything she wanted to be at that school. Every boy wanted her, every girl wanted to be her, or at the very least be her best friend if that was the best they could do. Even the teachers, male and female, seemed to be hypnotized by her charm. Jason even swore that he had caught a couple of the younger male teachers staring at her in inappropriate ways at times. Not that he could blame them. After all, they were only human too.

And the most amazing thing about Jennifer, aside from the way she looked in her brand-new full-length cheerleading uniform, was that she knew that she was the center of everyone's attention. And yet, she never acted like it. She was amazing. She could sit with the coolest kids in the school, yet she could sit with the kids that literally *no one* would be seen with, and no one seemed to care. Other than those poor souls with whom she sat with occasionally that no one else would sit with. To those kids, it was adding meaning to their otherwise unhappy and ostracized high school existence. And it meant everything! Truly, if Jen were to suddenly stand up one day and start walking on water, Jason would have been surprised, but not greatly. Probably just more amazed that she allowed anyone else to notice her doing it. She was just that down to earth and incredible.

He wasn't sure how long his trance lasted this time, but he judged that it had to have been quite a while. And frankly he just didn't care. She was worth the extra time. All of a sudden, his heart jumped into his throat and locked up so violently he didn't know if he'd be able to take his next breath. The jolt that shook him from his trance was her eyes. She had locked onto him with those beautiful, sparkling green eyes of hers. He couldn't actually see them given the distance between them, but he had seen them often enough that they were forever burned into his memory. She smiled and waved her megaphone in the air, which she had momentarily borrowed from her male counterpart behind her, as if gesturing to him. He raised his arm slightly to wave back at her, but just as quickly caught himself and pretended to scratch the back of his head. He felt like a fool. She never even knew he was there. Her gaze was unfocused. She was merely cheering. She never even saw him. She looked right through him. He knew the gaze well. He had seen it many times in the past.

As she turned away, his throat unlocked, and he gulped in a great deal of the fresh night air. He could smell the salt air from the ocean. The school was still a good distance away from the water, but nothing on Key West was too far from the ocean it seemed. The last lights of the dying sun were now getting smaller and dimmer as the evening closed in and the sun's last rays completely faded away. It seemed like an awfully good, yet devastatingly depressing simile for the way his senior year was closing out. The lights were fading quickly. He fervently hoped that next year was going to bring a new and brighter dawn for him. That was the best thing about hope. If it didn't work out next year, he always had the year after that to hope again.

He tried hard to forget about Jennifer as he turned back to his original destination, mentally trying to will his palms to stop sweating. He grabbed the hand rail and swung up onto the second step and started up the long walk to where his parents sat. The sad thing was that the walk was not truly that long and Jason knew it. A mere 25 rows separated him and his folks. It was *who* occupied the 25 rows between him and his parents that made the trek so nightmarish.

As he moved quickly up the stands, two rows at a time, he did his best to keep his eyes down as if focused on not missing a stair. The steps flew by as he practically ran straight up. His eyes would dart briefly to his left as he hit each new row, just long enough to see who the last two or three people of each row were, but not long enough to allow them to make eye contact with him.

He smiled sheepishly to himself groaning on the inside at how ridiculous he was acting. None of these people offered any type of danger to him. The same mix of people that had faced him this morning in the school hall and on the way into the ballgame, confronted him now in the stands. The danger was different here though. Here, he was confined. Here, there was no escape. The crowds were packed in like sardines. If he stopped for a second, if someone pulled him into a seat to talk to them, then he would panic. He would be worse than just trapped, he would be trapped into having to converse with people. His heart began palpitating at the mere thought. He would have to try to be funny, entertaining, intelligent, engaging. Everything that served to make him panic.

Jason was a strange combination of personalities. He wanted so badly to be accepted, to be one of the "cool kids," but he hated having to talk to people. It was not the people that he disliked; it wasn't even the conversations; it was the need to be "on" all the time. It took *effort* for Jason to be funny or interesting in the same way that his father could be at the drop of a hat. He did actually have the ability at times, but he knew that the stars had to align for it to happen for him. When Jason was "on" he could hold a conversation with most people and even impress them. The problem was that in order to be "on" he had to prepare for the situation. It took effort! Some people decide what they're going to say to a girl when they pick up a phone to call her. Other people spend hours preparing what they're going to say to a girl before they pick up the phone to call her. If she says this, then I'll say that. And God forbid, after all of that difficult planning and preparation, if the conversation went off topic, everything could be ruined!

Jason was usually pretty good at keeping on target with what he wanted to get out when he had a scripted "conversation" that he had created. The problem was that he needed that script. Rarely could he shine without deciding in advance what he would talk about. It didn't matter if the topic was weather and a hurricane was hitting at that precise moment. If he hadn't scripted it out in his mind, then he was useless. The hurricane could have been tearing the town apart right where he stood, but if he had not pre-planned the discussion, he was a dud. He would literally be frozen with fright and not be able to come up with a single thing to say. It really made no sense.

That was why this run was so difficult. He did not have anything prepared in case someone grabbed him and pulled him into a discussion. There were just too many different people to have conversations ready to go for all of them.

Sometimes he would actually stop in the middle of a conversation to think about what he wanted to say. People would stare, start talking without him or just walk away. His paralysis was taken for something else. He didn't even know what. He was pretty certain that each individual took it in their own way. Some probably thought he was aloof. Others, an asshole. Still others probably just thought that he was "off" or even a little bit slow. Who knows? Maybe they thought he was a lot slow. All Jason knew was that he hated it. He hated the way people stared at him. He hated the way they reacted. He hated *being* in those positions. He felt as if he were having a stroke when the fear seized him. So... his solution; avoid those "situations" at all costs.

He leapt up to the last row right before he would turn to move across to his parent's seats, and that's when it happened. "Jason!"

The attractive, not drop-dead gorgeous, yet definitely *very* attractive girl, Amy from his American History class yelled at him. She raised her arm and waived it excitedly to get his attention. Jason froze on the last step and turned slowly to look back at her. She was two rows down and only a couple of people in from the end of the row, yet she screamed as if she were on the other side of the field. He met her eyes and did everything he could to force a winning smile onto his face. A couple of other heads turned momentarily to look at him. They all instantly lost interest, either because it was just Jason or because he didn't do anything exciting in reply to her call to merit their continued interest. Either way, he didn't care, he was just happy that they lost interest.

Jason gave a nod of his head to Amy. "Hey, how you doin'? What's going on?"

"Hey come here." She waived excitedly again to emphasize that she wanted him to move into the crowd and join her.

Jason hesitated for a moment before deciding that there was no graceful way to avoid the confrontation. He glanced wistfully over to where his parents sat. His mother caught his eye and smiled broadly as she waved at him. He inclined his head and waved back, pointing down at Amy and flashing his mother a finger indicating he would be over there momentarily. His mother glanced down to Amy still staring up at Jason expectantly. Now she smiled knowingly and waived back her understanding. He could read that look of satisfaction and relief on her face as if it were his own feelings reflected there. She really was a great mother. All she wanted was the same success for him that she knew that her husband had achieved. She wanted the best for her son. And Amy would certainly be a big step up for her son over his current squeeze, which of course was no one! And even if he did have one, it still would be a big step up for him. That was easy to know, because she was good-looking and popular. Way above his social standing!

Jason turned his attention back to Amy. Building up his courage, he made his way into the inner circle. As he moved past the last person and dropped unceremoniously into the seat next to Amy, he was immediately very aware of how close his body was to hers. Again, she wasn't gorgeous, but she was still a very attractive girl. And if there was one thing that Jason did not have much familiarity with, it was attractive women this close up.

She put her hand on his shoulder and almost caused him to faint. "Jason, you've already completed that ridiculous end of the semester American History project, right?!?"

"Wh- what?" Jason started to stammer as he tried to get his wits back around himself again. "The American History project?"

Amy stared at him as if he had lost his mind. "Yeah, you know that one that I'm talking about. The one with the presidents and you have to make a newspaper article from the time period where a president has to argue or something about why he should be president. And then you have to figure out if they kept their promises... or something like that. You know I'm terrible with that history stuff. What do I care what they promise to get elected? My dad says they all lie anyhow." Amy kept talking at this point, but now Jason was just focused on one thing. She was pressing up against him as the crowd moved and reacted to their surroundings. He could feel her body press against his side as her arm slid a little bit around his back. He began to sweat as his arm moved slightly behind her back, pretending to stabilize himself as they swayed gently.

"Jason!"

"What?" Jason bolted back from his trance.

"Are you listening to me or just trying to cop a feel?" She laughed lightly and continued on as if she had just asked if it was raining. "So, will you help me with my project or what? I'll be eternally grateful to you if you do." Amy only lived two blocks over from him, so it was actually perfect. He had helped her with her homework many times before but it had been a while. They had lost touch over the last year or so due to having different classes and after school schedules, but she had always seemed very pleased to see him whenever they did see one another. He knew at the moment that she was just using him to do the work that she couldn't or didn't want to do, but he didn't care in the least bit. And doing the homework for her was perfect because it gave him lots of talking "material" to work with. He seemed to be funnier and more relaxed when he had some type of a crutch like that to work with.

"Yeah. Yeah," he laughed nervously, suddenly ginning up a little confidence. "Of course, you know I'll come over and help you. I like history projects like this. And," he swallowed as he took a leap, "you know I like working with you. You make it fun."

She giggled and slapped him playfully, "Oh, cut it out. Talk like that and my parents won't let me shut the door to my room when you're in there." She looked up at him giving him an exaggerated look of something more, but he knew she really was flirting with him and not mocking him. Or at least he was pretty certain anyhow. Even though she was definitely in a class above him, he thought that one day there was a chance that something might really happen. Funny, cool, attractive, he would certainly be lucky if it did happen. He wasn't counting his chickens yet, still...

They chatted for a few more moments about this or that, and even without his "prepared" material he seemed to do really well. They laughed about a couple of things before he started to make his departure. "Sorry Amy, I really gotta run. My mom and dad are waiting up there for me."

Amy looked up to where his parents sat, almost as if she had to confirm they were there in order for her to believe his story. "Well that's fine. But," she stuck her finger into his face in order to emphasize her point, "I'm going to see you at Jim's on Sunday night, right?!"

He backed up instinctively from her finger. "Jim's what?" He couldn't react fast enough to mask his surprise at the question.

"Oh, come on, seriously? How could you not know about Jim's party this weekend? Even the geeks know about it!" He reflected inwardly on the great news that that comment held for him. He wasn't considered one of the geeks. At least, not in her mind anyhow.

"Oh. Oh yeah, Jimmy's party. Yeah, yeah," he stammered, trying to get back on stride. "Yeah, I think I'm planning on going to that..."

"It's on Sunday," Amy filled in helpfully for him.

"Yeah. Oh yeah, I knew that," Jason kept stammering slowly. "I just, uh, just need to check with my parents, that's all." It was a weak ending, but he really didn't have anything else to fall back on. He really didn't believe her comment that even the geeks knew about Jimmy's party, but still... How did he not know about it?

"Ok Jason. You check with them." She leaned in to him and wrapped both arms around his waist now and gave him a little peck on the cheek. "I just want to make sure you know that you're going to be missing out if you don't show up there." She gave him another squeeze and pressed her cheek against his chest as she hugged him, before she let him go. Sitting there with his mouth open, she pretended to shoo him away. "Go on. Go ahead. Run and check with mommy and daddy to see if you can go," she teased him in an endearing manner. "Just don't forget that *I'll* be there." She winked to him before she turned back to her girlfriends who sat on the other side of her pretending not to notice their conversation. If he had been fooled by their act before he certainly wasn't when he looked back after having made his way back to the stairs. He turned back and caught the girls glancing at him and then quickly glancing away and giggling like the little school girls that they were. And for once, he didn't feel like they were making fun of him. He could tell that Amy really was interested in him and that her girlfriends were encouraging her.

He couldn't believe it. Jason smiled in a big way and bounded up the next couple of steps to make his way across to where his parents sat. He had trouble looking where he was going as he kept trying to glance back to see if Amy or her girlfriends would turn back around. All of a sudden, all of his butterflies and angst were gone. Amy was interested in him! There was no doubt about it. He was flying across the stands now as if he were being carried. He burst through the group and ended up almost tripping on top of his dad.

"Jason!" His dad's big voice boomed out in joy. "There's my big man!" His dad practically leapt up to embrace his son in a sincere, heartfelt bear hug. Everything his dad did, he did with great enthusiasm. "What are you up to tonight, sport?" His dad smacked him strongly on the back with his open hand as if he had just won the championship football game and deserved congratulating.

Life was good all of a sudden. Why not go for it! "Well, dad... Not much tonight. But on Sunday, Jimmy's having a party and..."

He couldn't even get the rest of the words out of his mouth. "Now that's my boy! A real party animal, just like his dad." His dad was beaming with pride. Had he just told him that he was MVP of the big game, he didn't think his father would have been any prouder. "You will definitely be there, and you will have a great time! But hey..." his dad paused for dramatic emphasis, "you be careful out there with the ladies now. You'll have to be back by 1 AM at the latest."

His dad knew he didn't have to worry about Jason breaking curfew. Jason hadn't ever done anything wrong like that in his life, although sometimes he thought his dad wished that he would. Jason knew he was saying it out loud and in a very boisterous manner specifically, so people *would* hear him warning his son, as if it was something that he had to worry about.

"Hey, is Amy going to be there?" Now his dad was craning his neck looking down to see if the girls were still looking up in this direction.

"That's the one you said he was talking to, right dear?" His dad tried to turn toward Jason's mom for confirmation, but he still hadn't spied Amy yet, so instead he just ended up contorting his head in a weird angle.

"Dad!" Jason almost shouted in exasperation at the spectacle his father was making. Catching himself, he quickly lowered his voice and put his head down. "Dad, please. You're embarrassing me!" Jason said fiercely in a whispered voice.

"Oh, come on son. You kidding me? She's a heck of a good-looking girl. I'd be yelling it from the rooftops if I was going somewhere with that young lady. Tonight, tomorrow, Sunday or any other night for that matter." And he meant it too. He made it very obvious to everyone that he had married the best looking, most intelligent and best loved woman in town. Jason didn't know if his mother had officially won any of those titles, but if you asked his father, he certainly would swear that they were all true. Beyond just enjoying showing off though, Jason knew that his father really did love his mother. He doted on her hand

and foot. That part wasn't macho enough for his dad, so he didn't show that off as much, but everyone in town pretty much knew that to be true as well. They worked well together. Jason often wished to one day have half the marriage that his parents had. And, to be considered in their class as parents, as well. He could not have asked for a better upbringing.

Finally, he couldn't hold back any longer. His father was still going on about how great Amy was and there was no longer any good reason to resist. Smiling sheepishly, Jason grumbled through his teeth. "Yes dad, Amy wants me to go to Jimmy's party."

"Now that's what I'm talking about!" His dad clapped him on the back again. Standing up in a flash, his father now yelled down to Amy, "Don't worry Amy, Jason will be there. I guarantee it!"

Jason about had a stroke. The whole place turned to stare up at his father and Jason's beat red face with his mouth completely open. His mother sitting next to his father with a big smile on her face. "Would you stop it, you big oaf.

You're embarrassing your son." She reached out and smacked him in the stomach.

Jason's dad grabbed his stomach as though really hurt by the fake blow. Even doubled over in pretend pain, he kept on talking, "Alright now, you go easy on him Amy, he's very fragile. I have to sit down now, but you kids have fun…, oww." His last statement cut short at the end with another, harder yet still playful shot from his mother.

Jason could barely look, he was dying with embarrassment, but when he did, he saw something amazing. Amy was standing up and staring directly at him. "You heard your dad Jason. You better be there." And then she was gone. Disappeared back into the stands to giggle with her girlfriends again. Jason was not entirely sure what had just happened.

"See son." Jason turned still in shock, mouth still wide open. "You just have to be a little bit forward with these good-looking ladies. Show them that you're in charge. That's how you get their attention. That's how I got your mom's attention."

"Oh, it was not, you big oaf. I just felt sorry for you is all."

Now they were playfully joking around with each other and absorbed in their own lives again. His dad immediately returned to telling another story. Jason sat and watched the game on the field in front of him. So few people ever actually came to watch the game he thought. Why would they however, when there were so many more interesting things going on in the rest of the world. And then his dad was back.

"Oh man! Jason did you see that!?! Did you see how the back just hit that hole! Like a battering ram that kid. He could probably play at one of those big schools up north. He does that night after night." Jason looked out onto the field. It was getting dark as night fell and it was tougher now to follow the action, but it had been a good run. As for playing college somewhere, Jason knew every bit as well as his father, that there was no way that would happen. The island hadn't had any players that Jason ever knew of move on to the big leagues and there probably wasn't anyone around that Jason saw that would break that trend. The running back on their team was a good player, but definitely not the type who could make it in the college ranks. He wasn't even the best runner in South Florida. There were rumors of a really good player up in Miami, but they hadn't gotten the chance to see him play yet, nor would they most likely get the chance. There was talk that he might be playing in college one day. But not any of the running backs that they were watching. No way, thought Jason.

"Boom! Look at him hit that line." His dad jabbed him with his elbow. His father loved high school football season. He would have loved it more if Jason had been out there, but they both knew that was impossible too. Jason might be able to turn things around with the ladies one day, maybe even on Sunday with Amy at Jimmy's party if things went well. His gaze turned involuntarily in her direction as he thought about it, but he knew with the utmost of certainty that he could never turn things around with his athleticism.

His dad interrupted his thoughts again. "Hey, how about this storm that I've heard talks of? Do I need to be worried about you getting back home Sunday evening before this thing hits the island?"

"Daaad." Jason threw an exaggerated look at his father. "Come on, be serious! No one is even talking about this thing. I haven't heard of any warnings. No one is concerned about it. It isn't even supposed to hit until Tuesday. I heard they were going to have a hurricane party over at Billy's if it gets strong enough and they cancel school for it."

"Yeah, well you can forget about that! I'm all for Jimmy's on Sunday, but starting bright and early Monday morning, we're battening down the hatches."

"Uh huh." Jason rolled his eyes. They would probably waste all day on Monday preparing, and the "storm" wasn't even supposed to be coming until Tuesday. Plus, they didn't even think it would hit the Keys according to everything he was hearing. Sheesh, Jason thought. Parents always overreact to everything.

5:07 PM, Saturday August 31st, 1935

2 days until the hurricane

"Mike!" The man saying his name in a manner that exemplified stress of the highest magnitude, strode purposely toward him in a very brusque way. "Mike, have you seen this report?" Tom waved the report he was holding in his hand emphatically. "It says there is a hurricane headed straight for the bottom of Florida."

The two men faced each other tersely in the small, sweaty office building in Miami, Florida. The fans on the desks were blowing furiously, but it seemed that their only purpose was to move the heat around the cramped, little office. Sweat poured down both of their faces. Mike wiped away some of the beads from his forehead, but Tom was too anxious to even notice his own perspiration mounting precipitously on his brow.

Mike pulled the bulletin from his characteristically, overly exuberant subordinate's hand. "Let me see what we've got here..." Mike looked at the bulletin with a grim look on his face.

This was a new one. They had been on the phones all day, "enjoying" a beautiful Saturday afternoon indoors in the sweltering heat instead of outside in the sweltering heat on the beach with his family where he wanted to be. All sorts of "experts" were giving their varied opinions on where this depression was heading and how much or how little it was going to grow. Someone in a building much nicer than theirs had decided that they needed to be on call today. Mike couldn't figure out why though. Not one expert agreed with another. So far they hadn't figured out a thing except that August in Miami was really freaking hot when you should be outside enjoying a three day weekend.

8-31-1935

152831 Advisory three thirty p.m. Key West wind direction = NW, velocity = 11mph. tropical disturbance of small diameter central near Long Island Bahamas apparently moving westnorthwestward attended by fresh to strong shifting winds and squalls possibly gale force near center.

Caution advised Bahama islands and ships in that vicinity. Norton NAR 3:40pm

"Hmm... You're right. This does not look good at all. Alright, Tom, let's get this out on the wire right away."

"On the wire!?! That's it? What about the radio and on TV? How about canvassing door to door? How about ordering the start of an evacuation?" Tom gestured and waved his hands around wildly. "We need to be getting the word out as quickly as possible. Those people down there deserve to be warned. We need to start organizing rescue crews to get down there in case this gets really bad."

"Tom, calm down." Mike turned around as he spoke and moved toward the other end of the office. "We don't even know if this is going to turn into a severe hurricane yet or not. Come on man. You can read this bulletin as well as I can. It's still way out there near the Bahamas, it's moving slowly and it hasn't even organized yet. It's just 'caution advised.' A 'tropical disturbance.'

For all we know it's not even going to touch on the…"

"Mike, are you blind?" Tom reached out and grabbed his superior's arm as he walked away and spun him around to face him again. One withering look from Mike and Tom immediately let go of his arm. Tom was always willing to fight his boss on just about anything, but when it came right down to it, Mike had been doing this for many years longer than Tom and was, quite frankly, still the unquestioned master of all things weather related in their little realm. Gathering his determination about himself again, however, he continued his verbal assault. "How can we not warn people about this? We need to get the word out immediately. If we just…"

"Tom!" Mike used his authoritative voice. His subordinate bit his lip hard, but stopped talking. "Enough. If it organizes more and moves closer, then we'll get the bulletins out there for real; we'll make the calls, we'll put it out via the radio and every other means of communication that we have available. We'll organize all the rescues and utilize all of the resources that we could possibly need. We have plenty of time. There's no reason to panic unnecessarily. And we aren't going to panic the public unnecessarily either. This is an '11 mph tropical disturbance with strong winds.' Not exactly the worst storm we've ever faced. You do this all the time, Tom. Let's not blow this out of proportion like you do with every other little wind storm that develops. Now," Mike spoke slowly and patiently as if addressing a wound-up child, "where's the Overseas Railroad at this moment?"

Tom stood silently for a moment clenching his jaw deciding whether or not to press his luck. Finally, he chose the prudent route and angrily muttered his words. "I think it just made its last run for the day. It should be returning to the islands tomorrow in the morning and then will be back here early in the afternoon."

"Perfect. If anything comes up, we can alert the rail and they can organize a rescue. Will that satisfy your frayed nerves?" It was phrased as a question and in a semi-jestful manner in order to break the tension, but it came out tersely and with no humor behind it. Tom knew that it brooked no serious answer however. Mike had already turned away and was almost seated at his desk when Tom finally responded.

"Aye-aye Captain," he responded sarcastically, adding quietly in a bitter whisper, "But I hope you know what you're doing!"

Mike didn't lift his head, but he brought his eyes up under his brow to see the back of Tom as he moved away. He had heard both comments. Lowering his eyes back, his own shoulders sagged. He couldn't let Tom see it, but he was worried too. It wasn't often that Mike would bring Tom and any of his team in on a Saturday, but this deserved some attention. The suits in the nicer building seemed to know something. It really was nothing more than a small squall at this particular moment in time, but it seemed poised to grow. Truly this wasn't a problem yet, but it certainly could be... And sooner than he wanted to admit!

And if it went sideways...

9:02 PM, Sunday, September 1st, 1935

1 Day until the Labor Day Hurricane

Jason strolled down the street slowly, almost lazily, simply enjoying the large soft raindrops that fell on his upturned face. He thought about his father worrying over the approaching storm and smiled. Having a three-day school week would be nice, he thought. These storms blew through here all the time. Lots of rain, tons of wind, swollen roads that made the cars impossible to drive around with their thin wheels and poor construction. Even the newer models that the wealthy families brought down from the big production plants up north had so much difficulty with the poorly constructed roadways that they rarely came out for days, sometimes weeks after the bigger storms soaked the islands. There was simply no way of draining the roads in an efficient manner. They were definitely going to get Tuesday off for this one too! He could tell already. Jason looked down and stomped his feet in a large puddle, enjoying the way the water flew in every direction. There was no denying that he was in a good mood after his brief encounter with Amy at the football game on Friday, a *very* good mood. Since then however, from the minute he had gotten up from sitting with his parents at the game on Friday night, he had been swamped. In fact, he had been so busy all day yesterday and all day today too, that he hadn't even gotten a chance to talk to her since then. But that was probably a good thing. The party should be a good "staging ground" for him, with lots of things to talk to her about. Still though, there was nothing that said definitively that the evening was going to go the way he planned or hoped it would. And yet, he was keenly aware of the lack of butterflies in his stomach at that moment. His smile broadened in the creeping darkness.

He stared wistfully at the beautiful houses that lined the street as he walked along the now muddy road. No one was on the roads and the island seemed entirely deserted. A couple of the houses had lights on within, casting faint glows from the shaded windows, the only sign of human activity. The homes on this street as with most streets in Key West were occupied by wealthy people from the industrialized north who had come down south from the 'frozen tundra' up that way to live in the still "untapped, untamed paradise of Key West". This beautiful, mostly, pristine area could not last much longer as it was. Or at least that was what his father always moaned about. With Henry Flagler's amazing new "8th Wonder of the World," people would continue to rush down to experience and explore their once well-hidden personal paradise. Already the mix of the islands was beginning to be felt, with more "poor" people being able to afford to move down here. Or even just shoot down to the bottom of the world for a quick visit. It seemed that "the Keys" as most people outside of the islands called them, were starting to become popular with the masses as well.

And yet, his father did not dislike the train. No one who lived in the Keys disliked it. It was an amazing accomplishment, and more specifically, it was *our* amazing accomplishment.

Still, an island that in many ways remained pristine and mostly undisturbed by the outside world, already had a total occupancy of more than

Tampa, Miami and Jacksonville put together and then doubled. It was quickly turning in to a very densely occupied locale. Many islanders preferred the status of being home to the elite wealthy, the not so elite or wealthy conch natives, the naval base and not much else. The military was a source of pride as much as anything else on the island. It was an odd combination of pride in isolation and pride in its countries amazing achievement that funneled new inhabitants into the area by the droves. The two thoughts were entirely in contrast to one another, yet inescapably intertwined.

Jason stared up at the large trees leaning in over the road that blocked much of the sky above from his view. The tranquil native palms were tall and spread wide at the top, reminding Jason of giant umbrellas providing the island with shade and a modicum of protection from the scorching sun when midday summers were at their worst. And the impressive Banyan trees showcased the amazing trunks winding in and out, this way and that, to create the most incredible climbing experiences that a young man could ever imagine.

As he continued to stroll down the street, he realized the rain had started to lighten up a bit. Up ahead he heard a young girl's voice rise above the peaceful quiet in a fit of youthful, uncomplicated laughter. He couldn't tell who it was for sure, although he was pretty certain that he would know all of the people who showed up to Jimmy's party tonight. Even though he was not known for frequenting these types of parties, he still heard the talk in school about who did attend and what wild events they had "supposedly" taken part in. A lot of what was repeated the next school day was as much made up as it was real, if not much more on the "made up" side. Of this, he was pretty certain that even the most gullible were aware. Still, they were usually pretty good stories, entertaining at the very least and they gave him a lot of material for his regular daydreams of grandeur. He had always secretly wanted to be one of the "heroes" of one of those great tales of bravado, although hero was probably not the best term to describe them.

Jason stopped for a moment, hidden in the dark shadows between the trunks of some larger banyan trees huddled off to the side of the road at the bend onto Jimmy's street. He placed both of his hands over his face and scrubbed at his eyes and cheeks as if trying to push his courage into his body or maybe to scrub away the fear that was always close at hand and ready to sap his courage. Either way, as his fingers slipped down over his eyes and he stared above them down the street to Jimmy's house, he silently reiterated his mantra of the night. "You are as good as any of them, Jason. You can do this. Don't be afraid. Talk to any of them. Be funny and be friendly, but don't back down. You belong here!" Even he wasn't certain if he believed the last part, but he told himself so in spite of himself. He did it because he had to make himself believe it!

Dropping his hands to his sides, he took one last long deep breath, shook the tension out of his shoulders and stepped back out into the center of the street to make purposely for his destination.

Jason reached for the door knob and, even as he turned it and pushed inward, he almost felt enough of his courage dissolve that he considered for a brief moment turning to run. His hope was that no one would have seen him yet and he could have made his get-away unnoticed. But then it was too late, or so he thought. The door was open, and he had stepped gingerly inside. For a moment a couple of the nearest people to him turned and looked to see who it was. As soon as they realized it was just him however, they immediately went back to their self-absorbed lives. As he reflected for a moment, he thought, maybe they aren't "self-absorbed." Maybe they just weren't interested in anything he had to offer. Or maybe their turning to look at him was his opportunity to do something and he let it pass without seizing the moment. But that didn't necessarily mean that they were only interested in themselves, did it?

Shaking his head briefly to clear it, he refocused on the moment at hand. Regardless of their personal situations, Jason was very accustomed to this typical type of dismissal of himself. He posed no prospect of interest for them. And as it turned out, he still could have run in that instant and he doubted that anyone would have been any less the wiser. Maybe someone would have remembered 'thinking' they had seen him at the party, but he doubted that anyone would actually really remember him being there.

Shrugging it off, remarkably quickly he suddenly realized, he straightened his shoulders, lifted his head high and strode purposely into the room, even pretending to greet someone who hadn't really even noticed him yet. The ruse worked fairly well though, he noted, as this time a couple of people did actually seem to notice him.

His initial air of excitement dissipated as rapidly as it had coalesced. Five minutes into the party, he had now taken a few laps around the house and had already exhausted the number of times he could nod with indifference to the same people. He began to feel the fear welling up inside of him. His chest started to constrict. It seemed like it was becoming harder to breathe suddenly. He began to glance around frantically, hoping that no one was watching him. He needed to speak to someone. He needed to do something. He had to have a purpose for why he was standing there. Fortunately, and unfortunately, for Jason however, no one showed any signs at this point of even realizing that he had ever existed, let alone that he was standing in the center of the room with them in plain sight experiencing a panic attack that had completely immobilized him. An attractive girl that sat behind him in one of his math classes last year, or perhaps it was the year before, he honestly could not remember which, walked past him and gave him a once-over-glance that told him all he needed to know. She dismissed him more easily than if he had been a dying fern planted in the corner of the room. He smiled lamely at her, overly conscious of the fact that he realized he had nothing to say to her and no move to make. She was gone with a slight swish of her long, beautiful hair.

He desperately wanted, no *needed,* someone to speak to. He was too self-conscious just standing there. All of a sudden, he felt like he had absolutely nothing to say to anyone here. All of his brilliantly thought out conversations that he had practiced a dozen times on his way over here, had escaped, flying off in the humid, warm island air. Nothing was left except for fear and a tight clenching of his chest. His heart pounded, and his hands began to sweat. He glanced around wildly looking for something to grab onto. Some person he could speak to, or some action he could take to give himself a sense of purpose. He needed something. He secretly *begged* for something. Anything!

Without even knowing what he was doing, he abruptly broke into action. Jason turned so swiftly he almost knocked a beer out of another girl's hand who had just walked up behind him with her boyfriend in tow. He knew them both instantly, Tina Johnson and Bob Wilson. They were known around school as the "cutest couple in school". They did everything together. And to tell the truth, they were both pretty nice. Neither one of them had ever said a mean word to Jason, or anyone else for that matter. He smiled awkwardly, as he always did, mumbled his excuse for not paying attention to where he was going and then was gone.

Sadly, it never even dawned on Jason that they had been walking up to chat with him. Bob wanted to know why they hadn't been seeing him around at any of the parties and Tina was dying to know what was happening with him and Amy.

Completely clueless to any of this though, and impossible for him to even assume that they might be interested in him, he was gone before they could even engage him.

Where he ended up after leaving the bewildered, "cute" couple behind was the bathroom. As it happened, there finally was no line at the door. He bolted in and slammed the door shut behind him. Sighing, he let his head sag against the solid, wooden door. Then he pulled his head back and banged it once or twice against the door for good measure. He actually grimaced as he pulled back and rubbed his head, a little surprised at how hard the door was.

Turning to the mirror, he placed his hands squarely on the beautiful, yet faux ornate bathroom countertop and stared angrily into the reflection that glared back at him.

"Dammit!" He scowled angrily at himself again. "This is *not* how it's going to go down tonight! I am better than this! I am going to go out there and I'm going to entertain. I'm going to be witty. I'm going to be the life of the party. Whatever I need to do!"

He squeezed the countertop and pushed off as if determined not to waste another second. Snapping the cold water handle to the "on" position, he splashed some cold water onto his face. As he dragged his fingers across his face, he paused when his eyes came into view again and he saw his reflection once more. As if staring himself down, he glared menacingly at himself once more. He felt like he was going into battle or something, possibly to his death. And for Jason, humiliation was about as good as death. Or maybe worse!

Wiping his face dry brusquely with a hand towel, he turned, grabbed the bathroom door handle and took one last deep breath. Putting on his game face he swung the door inward and almost slammed into two girls who stood outside just beyond the door.

"Amy?!" Jason felt as if the word was ripped from his mouth. He meant to say something else, but nothing else emerged from his open mouth.

"Have I left you speechless for a second time this weekend, young man?" she teased adorably, laughing at the way he stood motionless with his mouth hanging open.

"Uh, oh, no. Ah, I was just finishing up in there and... and didn't expect you out here..." He gestured back to the bathroom and then back at Amy, before closing his eyes in total embarrassment as he realized what he had just said.

"Well, I would have waited inside with you, but you didn't invite me in." She giggled as she made a show of rubbing her body slightly against his as she pushed her way into the bathroom. Her friend Julie, who was now tagging along, also slid into the bathroom, but Jason was very conscious of how she did not make any contact with him, but *Amy certainly had!* They laughed loudly as Amy put her hands on his waist and gently moved him outside the bathroom and closed the door.

Jason, squeezing his eyes shut and making fists as he berated himself for his ridiculous comments, was surprised when the door opened back up unexpectedly a second later.

Amy stuck her head back out. "You're going to be ok until I get out, right?" She paused for effect as he turned around and stared at her in confusion. "Well, I just know that tonight's going to be your night to *be witty, to do anything necessary, to do whatever it is that you need to do!*" She giggled uncontrollably and raising her eyebrows at him, she disappeared back into the bathroom to more peals of laughter from within.

Oh my God. He could not have been that loud in there. Could he...?

The night could not have started out any worse.

Walking woodenly back into the kitchen area like a zombie, he saw a rare sight. There was an open chair at the tiny, little table where everyone had been playing some drinking games. Jason did not play drinking games. But tonight, he was not Jason. Something within him snapped. Something changed. All of a sudden, he was someone completely different. He was someone wild, someone uncontrollable and someone unexpected. He screwed on a face of courage and without asking or thinking, he jumped into the chair. "What are we playing and what are we drinking?"

His voice didn't even sound like his voice. It was authoritative, it boomed with confidence. The three guys still at the table all whipped their heads up or around in unison. "What?" one of them managed.

"Come on man, what are we playing?" His hand shooting out to grab the glass in front of him, Jason continued, trying to get out all of the words before his mind could stop him. "What's this? We drinking beer or we got some moonshine here?"

The three boys exchanged glances. "Ah, hey… Jason," said the lead kid at the table, stuttering as he greeted him, clearly surprised by Jason's new tone and attitude. "You drink?" The kid, Tommy, a nice enough guy who was in the upper echelon of the cool kids, who had hung around with Jason from time to time when they were younger, asked. They definitely were not tight friends, but they talked on occasion and didn't go out of their ways to avoid each other. They had been closer friends when they had been younger, but they had drifted apart more and more as Jason had shied away from the limelight and Tommy had continued to be drawn to it.

"I do tonight, Tommy. Hit me man. What are we playing?" Jason repeated as his confidence grew. He reached out and grabbed the cards in front of him.

"Hey." Tommy grabbed the cards from Jason's hands. "Give me those. Those are Steve's from the last hand. We're starting again. Straight up poker. You know how to play, right?" Even though Tommy asked Jason, he knew full well that Jason knew the game. They had played lots of cards in the past, back when they had been closer.

"Good enough to whip your ass, Tommy! Let's go man, get those cards out there. And how about a beer over here?" Jason turned this way and that in his chair as if looking for a waitress. "What's a guy gotta do to get some service around here?"

The three kids at the table with him glanced back and forth between themselves still bewildered by the transformation in Jason's attitude, but then Tommy smiled broadly and bellowed, "Oh, well we'll just see about that Jay!" as he started throwing cards out on to the table.

And just like that, out of the clear blue, Jason felt like he was back. He was back in second or third grade when he was just a kid. Back when he just wanted to play and run and have a good time with his friends like Tommy. He didn't care back then who thought he was "cool" or "hip". All he wanted to do was to have a good time. Sure, back in second grade he didn't have a beer to drink, but otherwise, he felt every bit as free and just as loose.

At least an hour had slipped past as Jason kept putting down cards and beers. Finishing his second beer and half way through his third, it was beyond a doubt that the liquor was working its magic on him. Never one for drinking, he didn't need a whole lot to be pushed over the edge of sobriety. "What's with all of the noise over here?" Amy sidled up next to the table pushing her way through the tight ring of kids who had positioned themselves around the four boys and forcibly slid half a cheek onto the chair where Jason was sitting. Jason, now disoriented from the liquor and the heady experience of being the center of attention, was completely caught off guard by the powerful shove of Amy's hip on his. Without even a moment's time to make a grab for the table's edge, Jason went straight down to the floor with a crash. The kids were so tightly positioned around the table that he essentially caused a small chain reaction of kids tripping and swaying backwards on top of each other.

Falling off the seat with such a goofy look of utter shock, the place paused in unison for half a moment before everyone in the room burst out laughing. His beer haze having been broken for a brief moment by the surprise of the sudden upending, it allowed him to look up and give a slightly chagrined smile. Pushing himself back up, he slipped back onto one half of the chair and pressed himself up against Amy's leg. The feel of her body pressed so tightly against his made even more blood rush to his face... and other areas. The beer was not the only thing that was now causing his head to swim.

The next hour flew by. Everything he seemed to say was able to elicit the beautiful, enticing sound of laughter from Amy. The guys all continued to shout and cheer. It was a night that Jason was certain he was never going to forget.

The night kept getting later and the beer and cards kept on going. As drunk as he was though, Jason realized that the hour was getting later and later. It's gotta be time to go by now, he thought hazily. His brain was now shouting at him as he realized that he had just played two more hands since the last time he thought that he had to leave.

"Oh YEAH!" Jason slammed the cards down on the table with a big flourish throwing both hands up in the air in triumph. His cards revealed a full house and a victory. Smiling ear to ear he rose wobbly to his feet. "Yeah baby, look at that! Read 'em... and weep, boys!" He was having a lot of trouble now getting his words out, but he took great pleasure in the reactions that they caused when he did get them out. Two of the kids threw down their cards in disgust as they realized that their hands had lost, while the third, Tommy, still sat staring at his hand in a fog of alcohol-induced confusion trying to figure out what just happened.

Amy jumped up with a big grin on her face as well and clapped her hands together excitedly. "That's awesome, Jason!" She threw her arms around Jason's neck excitedly and planted a big kiss on his lips. Caught completely off-guard, Jason swayed and reacted slowly at first. But after the initial shock faded, he quickly embraced her back and leaned fully into the kiss.

All around him, there was action. People were talking, music was blaring, and people were doing things, but nothing was going through Jason's mind at that moment. Nothing was ruining the moment. He was in bliss. He was in heaven. All was forgotten. His head swam as he kissed the beautiful woman in his arms. His mind was weak and feeble from the liquor. Everything swam around him. Colors and sounds were jarring and indistinguishable. Nothing was able to break through the fog that enveloped him. He knew somewhere deep in his brain that he would never forget this night, and he fervently hoped that he would get to repeat it another time when he might be able to appreciate it a little more.

Suddenly, he noticed something. Something was different. He opened his eyes and realized that he was no longer making out with his beautiful new girlfriend, or at least he was hoping that's what she was. He looked into her face and abruptly comprehended that she was laughing at him. As the cloud lifted momentarily, he came to understand that he probably had not been kissing her for some time now. He had drifted off into one of his little dreamlands, but this one was alcohol enhanced, so it didn't really fall into the realm of one of his customary fantasy worlds. At least, not according to his scorecard anyhow.

He smiled as his head lolled to one side. "You are... *wasted*!" Amy over-emphasized the word as she laughed prettily at him. He let his head loll to the other side this time. As his head dropped heavily onto his chest, he realized that his brain had made the decision to finally leave. His brain barely registered the words as he swayed towards the kitchen door, practically falling through the opening. His hand reached out and narrowly caught himself in the nick of time as he stumbled further. Another moment more and he would have missed the wall entirely and gone straight down on his face, causing himself a lot of pain. Not that he would have felt it until the next morning, but he definitely would have felt it then.

Pushing off, he commenced stumbling through the living room this time and up to the front door where hours earlier this entire bizarre adventure down the rabbit hole had begun. For a moment, he swore that Amy was next to him, talking to him. But by the time he had turned to look for her though, she had faded away from sight. There was no sound of her gentle laughter or sight of her beautiful face. Everything was now a swirl of uninterrupted color and noise. Nothing stood out to him.

Finally, a face emerged from the blur of colors. Lou had been in the pack of guys, watching as Jason had exploded onto the scene. He had been every bit as much in awe of the transformation as everyone else. Enthralled by the renaissance of a boy they had all known as children growing up together yet could not recognize at the party. Lou had watched and wondered what had happened. Now he no longer cared. Now he just wanted to keep the good times rolling. Jason was a wild man tonight and Lou could easily see him as his wingman.

"Yo, Jason!"

Jason swung violently around in an awkward manner as he tried to locate the source of the latest intrusion through his alcohol clouded mind. He squinted his eyes and leaned forward, "Louuu...?" Jason slurred and extended his old friend's name in cadence with how he swayed.

Lou smiled broadly as he tried to determine if Jason was just saying his name in an exaggerated way as many of his classmates did, or if he was simply too smashed to say it properly. It took all of about three seconds, however, to realize that Jason couldn't say anything without screwing it up. Standing up seemed to be almost beyond his capabilities at the moment.

And yet, there he was staggering now in Lou's direction. A moment of guilt passed over Lou as he considered doing the right thing and making sure that Jason got home ok. It was just a moment though. "Come on, Jason. A bunch of us are headed out to the beach right now to kick this party into high gear. We've got beers, Johnny set up a bonfire already. It's going to be awesome."

"I dunno knoooo..." Something resembling words slipped from Jason's mouth as he reached out to grab Lou's shoulders in an effort to steady himself. Lou stared intently at Jason trying to make something out that his childhood friend was murmuring. "I... go. I... don't... go."

Not entirely certain what Jason had just mumbled to him, Lou decided to just answer him how he wanted to. "Of course you can go. Why couldn't you? We're just headed down to the beach. It's not like we're doing the chain gang and heading for the mainland."

Lou continued to talk at Jason, but he was no longer paying his friend any mind. Jason had never been invited to be part of the Chain Gang group, but then again, why would he be? In order to be in the group, you had to be willing to leave the islands without your parents' permission via the overseas railroad. No one would have bothered to invite him, because no one would expect him to say yes. That just wasn't who Jason was. At least, not until tonight anyhow. Or so Jason thought.

Even as he was thinking about how tonight would be his night to join the Chain Gang, he awoke from his stupor with a start. "Where?" His head swiveled around in an unfocused fog that told him nothing of his surroundings. "Where are we?"

"Where are we?!? What are you talking about Jay? I told you this is the back way to the beach. Have you even heard a word I've said?" Lou looked back at him for a moment suddenly aware that Jason hadn't heard a word. And sincerely had no clue as to what was happening. He grinned a little bit in the darkness. "What? Are you afraid of traveling off the beaten path a little bit?"

Jason stared around bewildered and befuddled at how he had gotten here so fast. He didn't recognize any of the trees or any of the homes. Jason knew his way around Jimmy's neighborhood, and this was definitely not it. He honestly didn't even remember having left Jimmy's house, let alone the entire neighborhood. But before he could even start to really try to figure out where he was, he stumbled and crashed to a knee just as they started to move in between two houses. Yelping in pain from the root that he struck, he automatically put his other knee down to support himself and tried to lean back so could grab his injured knee with both hands.

"Shush! What the hell's the matter with you?!?" Lou's tone was sharp and biting. Even drunk, Jason could hear the fear. Despite the admonition, a small hiss escaped through Jason's tightly gritted teeth. After a moment of sharp pain, it began to dull quickly. A bi-product of everything he had drunk that night he surmised in a dull fashion. As he gathered his feet under himself again with Lou's help, and started shambling forward, the realization dawned on him. Directly in front of him, on the other side of the homes, he could already tell stretched the beautiful, blue waters that encircled their perfect little island paradise. They were moments from the beach.

Apparently the next few hundred yards passed again without his knowledge since the next thing he saw was a huge bonfire crackling and smoking directly in front of him. Some kid he barely recognized from his math class screamed excitedly and threw his hands up in the air as the fire crashed in on itself shooting sparks high up into the night air above. One of his outstretched hands clutched a beer in it that he brought joyously to his lips for a long pull. "Woo!!! Now that's a fire!"

Drunk as he was, Jason managed to think to himself, well I guess we don't need to be quiet any longer. He swayed unsteadily on his feet as he smiled to himself at his funny little thought.

After a moment or two of standing still and his funny moment had passed, he decided he was ready to move again. Jason stumbled forward raising his hand to his eyes to shield himself from the sudden explosion of heat and light. He noted from the corner of his eye that Lou had wandered off to say hi to some of their friends from the party who had beaten them to the spot. Jason glanced around, wobbling as he did so, trying to figure out who he should speak to, or where he should go. In the end, just collapsing onto the sand right where he was standing felt like the best option.

He stared at the fire for a while and absently drank the beer that had appeared in his hand. Someone, he decided, was an angel for supplying him with the unnecessary but awesome gift of more beer. Lost in the beauty of the flames as they danced in front of him, he almost jumped out of his skin when Amy plopped down beside him and grabbed his hand in hers.

"Now this is just absolutely perfect!" She sighed contentedly as she leaned against his shoulder.

Jason was certain that the shock was written all over his face, fortunately she read none of it. She was staring at the magical flames just as contentedly as he had been only moments before. Her fingers absently ran across his as she sat unmoving, enjoying the moment.

Jason's head swiveled around, back and forth trying to see who might be paying attention.

He wasn't even sure if he was looking to see if anyone was observing how cool he was, or if he was looking to see if it was just the two of them. Either outcome felt perfectly fine to him at that moment.

"So…" Jason's head involuntarily moved back a bit as she surprised him again by lifting her head and turning abruptly towards him. Her finger landed perfectly on his lips as he started to speak.

"Don't."

He stared silently in surprise over her fingertip at her beautiful face.

"Don't say a word. I don't want you to ruin it. Guys say very silly things." She was speaking as calmly and patiently to him as if she were speaking to a child about why the sky is blue. "And *you* have been saying some really silly, stupid things lately."

"Me?!?" Now Jason smiled, even more shocked than he had been before. "What… what silly things… have I been saying?" Talking seemed

126

to be extremely difficult at the moment, especially with her finger still on his lips.

"A lot. Mostly since about the third or fourth grade. And...," She stared deeply into his eyes making him extremely conscious of how close her lips were to his, "I'm tired of it Jason Milner Johnson!"

"Ughh." Jason groaned rolling his eyes. He hated his middle name. And his last name too, to be honest. Could it be any more vanilla? Just like he was, plain and unexciting.

"See!" Amy exclaimed.

Jason refocused. "What?"

"I can tell. You're doing it right now, aren't you?" She stabbed an accusing finger towards him. "You're thinking about how you're not good enough for everyone around here. It kills me."

Standing up and moving away from him she began pacing back and forth in short small strides along some invisible line dusting sand off of her bottom angrily as she stomped. "You used to be so different. You used to be so much more confident. You used to be…" She stopped pacing now, grasping at the air with her hands and the words with her mind. She seemed frustrated and like she wanted desperately to get something across to him. But sadly, his continued beer-soaked stupor would not let him focus. All he could concern himself with was why she was no longer sitting next to him and pressing up against his body. He knew that he should be focused on her words, but her body had his mind so preoccupied elsewhere that no matter how hard he tried, all he could think about was her sitting next to him and kissing him again. In fact, he was so wrapped up in his thoughts about her, that he had missed anything else that she had just said and had not even realized that she was moving back towards him again.

But she was moving back towards him now, slowly. She was shuffling her feet in the sand again. "You're every bit as good as them you know." She spoke softly now, almost as if to herself instead of Jason. "I've been in love with you forever. It's just always killed me how little credit you give yourself."

"I… give myself… credit when… Wait a second. Did you just say you're in love with me?" Jason was sputtering along trying to get out something else that was comprehensible and hopefully, intelligent, when he was saved from that unlikely outcome by a yell from Lou.

"Hey, are you guys coming?" Lou walked up and took a swig from his beer as he looked at them quizzically.

"Coming where?" Jason slowly stood up, barely managing the task as his mind still struggled with Amy's last statement. When he finally managed the almost insurmountable task, he swayed slightly on his feet back and forth as he stared at Lou as if he had never met him before.

"We're headed to go see the storm," Lou gestured in no particular direction with his hand holding the beer. "I guess it's getting pretty big now according to some of the guys. Might be some good waves out there."

"Waves?" It was a question from Jason, although his mind was so addled at the moment, that he wasn't even one hundred percent certain what he was asking.

"Whoa, Jason. You ok?" Lou was looking at him closely now leaning in to get a better look at him as he moved forward toward his old friend. "You don't look so good..."

"He's fine, Lou." The irritated tone in Amy's voice caught Lou off guard for a moment.

Turning his head in her direction he recovered enough to speak to her. "Whoa, ok there Amy. Relax. I'm just trying to keep the good times rolling."

"Rolling? Rolling?!?" The tone in her voice now really began to freak him out. "You haven't kept the good times rolling with Jason since second grade. Where have you been for Jason?" Amy started advancing toward Lou with shoulders hunched forward and a determined look in her eyes.

Lou started backing up, stumbling as he moved away from the fire and her line of attack. His hands were slightly raised as if warding off an attacking menace. "Hey, I was just excited to see the old Jason back," he nodded slightly in the direction of his dazed buddy. "I just wanted to know if you guys want to go see the storm that's all."

Amy stopped her determined march and straightened up a bit as if trying to gain control of herself. "Sorry, Lou. I shouldn't be attacking you. I'm just angry at this big oaf over here."

Jason kind of half-smiled to himself as he swayed slightly back and forth in his semi-haze of confusion. It seemed as if people hadn't shown this much interest or concern for him in years.

"Well..." Amy spoke in a slow manner as if trying to determine whether or not she would like to head out to the beach. "This has been a good night for him so far. And I have seen some marked improvement." She raised one eyebrow and gave him a knowing look, which he completely missed of course. "And I would like to see a little more of this new, 'old' Jason. Who knows if he'll still wake up the same Jason tomorrow or not..."

Lou stood there staring at Amy as if he were witnessing an alien being for the first time. Finally, he gave up and exasperated he asked, "So... does this mean we're going to the beach or what?!?"

Amy never even looked at him. "Hey Jason." She now had the sweetest sounding voice. "Wanna go to the beach with me to watch the waves?"

Even in his addled state of mind, the question was the simplest, no-brainer he had ever been posed. "Uh huh." He shook his head slowly, never taking his eyes off the beautiful girl, who moments before had been berating him non-stop for being foolish.

As she took his hand and led him off the beach, following behind Lou, she whispered quietly in his ear with a coy, little smile. "Don't think for a second that we're done with our little talk though."

Inwardly, he groaned, as she gave his hand a gentle squeeze. Another beach... Great!

9:12 PM, Sunday, September 1st, 1935

1 Day until the hurricane

"Tom, GO HOME!" Tom stopped his pacing and turned to look at his boss. It wasn't an angry assertion, just a definitive one. Both men had put in long hours reading the reports and debating what their response to the developing crisis should be. "Tom," Mike paused and rubbed his dry, irritated eyes with his knuckles and sighed. "I know you're worried. I know you want to do something, but there is nothing that we can do right now. We've read every report; we've looked at every angle. We just don't know what this storm is going to do right now or if it's even going to continue to escalate. I can't just requisition the Flagler railroad without any concrete evidence that those people need to be evacuated. Plus, you know a lot of those people aren't going to leave their homes or stations even if we tell them to go. The soldiers need that money. They aren't going anywhere. The residents have been through these storms a thousand times and they almost always insist on "riding it out." So, they aren't going anywhere. It's a holiday weekend. We're all working when we should really be at home barbequing with our families. Everyone's stressed about this one. I get it." He paused for a moment to give Tom time to let the words sink in again, despite the fact that this was already about the fiftieth time today that they had had this same exact discussion. "I'm sure I don't have to remind you that we are in a horrible depression and the last thing that this area needs is the unnecessary use of very limited resources. We just can't afford this right now."

Tom stood perfectly still listening intently, knowing full well he had no chance of winning the argument. Regardless, he was not going to make it easy for his boss. Finally, he spoke, quietly, but in a tone that was just as definitive as his boss's tone had been. "I'll be back in here at 6 AM tomorrow." He leveled his gaze at his boss as if daring him to disagree.

Mike's shoulders sagged from relief. He was worried for a moment that his subordinate would actually disagree and continue the fight, as futile as the effort would have been. "Thank you."

Tom turned and slowly moved toward the door. He stopped with his hand on the door handle when he heard his superior's voice, "You know I'll be here too." Tom nodded slightly before turning the handle and pulling hard. And just like that, he was gone into the blowing winds and driving rains. Mike dropped heavily into the seat behind him and glanced down wearily one last time at the final bulletin of the night in his hands. His heart beat loudly in his chest. "God help me," he murmured as he crumpled the paper in his hands and shut his tired eyes.

9:17 AM, Monday, September 2nd, 1935

The morning of the Labor Day Hurricane

"Jason!" He immediately recognized the sharp biting tone of his mother's voice. She was *not* happy with him!

"Whaaaat? Mom?" Jason rubbed at his bleary, aching eyes. "What... how... did I get here?"

"Good question, mister. I was going to ask you that. But I think I'm just going to let your father deal with you. I can't even stand to look at you right now!"

He seemed to hear or sense his mother turn and move away from him. But he never saw the smile on his father's lips that died immediately when his mother whipped around to face him.

"And you...!" Jason's eyes were pressed shut against the light pouring into his room that seemed to be searing his brain, but all the same, he could just imagine his mother's accusing finger jabbing away mere inches from his father's nose. "You better not let him off easy."

Jason heard his father mumble something in assent as she slammed the door angrily behind herself.

"Wow." It had taken his father a few moments to speak after his mom had left his room. Jason wasn't sure if it was from fear of her hearing him speak or just that he was too dumbstruck to say something at first. When Jason finally cracked his eyes enough to see his father standing there, he saw that he was still staring rigidly after her with his hands on his hips. Eventually he swiveled his head around to face Jason with a boyish grin plastered back on his face again. "You really steamed her something good. She's ready for me to sacrifice you to the God of all that's holy." He chuckled quietly to himself seeming to enjoy some sort of a joke that he had just made that Jason was apparently not aware of.

Jason slowly shut his eyes again for a moment as the room started to spin once more.

"So?" Jason opened his eyes again, startled by his father's one word question, and the fact that his father was now perched precariously on the side of his bed staring intently at Jason's face with an eager expression. "Well," his dad whispered fiercely. "How'd it go?"

"Huh?" Jason was completely flummoxed now. He didn't think his father had moved that fast since his senior year playing football. Was this a trap? Was his father playing an angle or trying to trip him up? He wasn't sure. And he certainly wasn't going to answer until he knew better what was happening. "About what? How did what go?"

His father pulled back now with a stunned look. "Are you serious? You really don't know what I'm asking about?" His father stole a look back to the now closed door, as if concerned Jason's mother might fly in at any moment and catch him in the act of *not* scolding his son. "With Amy, you big oaf. How'd it go with Amy?"

"Amy?" Jason was getting a bit tired already of always being so confused, but there did not seem to be any end in sight to his utter and absolute lack of knowledge of pretty much everything that was occurring around him. "How did you know about Amy?"

"Son. I know it was a long time ago that your mother and I got married, and I haven't dated anyone since then. But I still know how the game is played. Any fool alive could have seen where you were headed last night. So... What happened?"

Jason looked deep into his father's eyes, and almost couldn't believe what he saw. His father was not proud of him. He was bursting with pride. Jason, a moment ago, assured of never seeing the sun again except from his room or school window, was suddenly aware of the fact that his father not only didn't want to scold him, he wanted to give him an award. Jason smiled a tired, but very happy smile. "It was great, dad!"

His dad sat up straight with a grin that every father hopes to share one day with his son and slapped him heartily on the shoulder. Nodding in a proud way, his dad spoke with a great deal of admiration, "Now that is what I wanted to hear!" But then half a beat later, he followed up with,

"You know I still have to ground you for a month though, right?"

Jason's only response was to roll over on his side, moan and puke all over the floor off the side of his bed.

Always with a sense of humor, although not always one appropriate for the situation, his father looked down at him and deadpanned, "Good talk son. I'll go get your mother..."

11:01 AM, Monday, September 2nd, 1935

Just over nine hours prior to the Labor Day
Hurricane's Landfall

Crew members and platform loading laborers scampered around in the light downpour as the Labor Day Excursion train, destined for Miami, arrived in Key West. They had been frantically preparing the mighty engine and cars to bring the holiday's celebrants back to the mainland in the hopes of finishing quickly so they could find a bit of shelter from the miserable weather. Essentially everyone there wanted to be somewhere else by this time. The travelers had none of the excitement and joy that they had experienced on the trip over. Now, they were simply tired. The long, wet weekend had ended, and they were headed back, most of them, to the real world of jobs and responsibility.

The train had required extra care on this particular day because it was being specially equipped with extra cars and a heavier crew than usual in order to handle the additional passengers that they had anticipated ahead of time to be heading home on this soggy morning. And aside from the fact that many of them had to leave in order to get back to work, who could blame them for wanting to leave. Due to the uncharacteristically bad weather, it had been one of the worst Labor Day weekends in recent memory on the beautiful, little islands.

The locomotive and the tender were moved to the opposite end of the train in preparation. The oil and water had been depleted and needed replenishing, as normally occurred on these trips. Still, even with the extra effort required due to the horrible conditions, it had been settled by noon, mostly because of the extra-large crew, and parked in position on a siding, quietly waiting for the passengers to file on board for their ill-fated trip.

12:13 PM, Monday, September 2nd, 1935

Just over eight hours prior to the Labor Day
Hurricane's Landfall

Pop, pop, pop... pop, pop. Jason suddenly whipped his head around at the unexpected sounds. Then, he immediately let out a loud, audible groan in protest over his stupidity. He definitely could not afford to move that quickly. He lifted his hand to the back of his neck and kneaded it roughly as he tried to make the new pounding behind his eyes dissipate.

He stopped for a moment, wondering now if perhaps he had imagined the sounds or if it was just a squirrel or some other nuisance animal outside his window. Then, he heard it again. And, this time he saw it. This time he was also more cautious in his investigation as to what was happening. Plus, now he had an idea of what was going on. Someone was throwing rocks or gravel at his second story window. Swinging his legs over the side of the bed, he stood up... slowly. Moving to the window, he pushed back the heavy curtain that only partially blocked his view to the outside world. Squinting as he looked down, it took him a moment for his eyes to adjust to the bright sun, but there they were. Lou, with another handful of gravel ready to chuck, and Amy, looking radiant as always. Lou looked disappointed as he let the remaining rocks fall from his hands and brushed them against his shorts.

Jason, quietly, he hoped, unlocked and opened his window. He didn't know if his mom was at home, but he knew that his father still was. "What are you two doing down there?" he asked, in a loud stage whisper. His voice croaked in his throat from the damage done by the mix of liquor, the poor sleep last night and the vomit this morning. He really was not feeling tip top.

"Three," Lou offered helpfully, in his own awful attempt at a whispered yell. "Julie's in the car waiting." Lou smiled big and gave the raised eyebrows of excited anticipation. "She's scared of your dad, but ready to hit it."

"Hit what?" Jason couldn't seem to remember the last time he was *not* confused by something that someone said to him.

"The beach, you big goofball. The waves are supposed to really be getting big now!" Amy smiled as she swung her hips back and forth slowly while standing in place. God, she had an amazing way of capturing his attention.

Lou waited as long as he could. "Seriously? Are we going or what?"

Jason started to reply, "But guys. After yesterday, I am soooo grounded... And my head..." Jason slowly raised his hand to his forehead as if to demonstrate the pain, but it didn't seem like either Amy or Lou noticed or cared.

In fact, Amy didn't even bat an eyelash. "So...?" The question just seemed to hang out there for an eternity. "Does that mean you are not coming...?"

It was incredible the way she had the power to make moments last for hours.

Jason was in shock. He hadn't climbed out the back of his house, down the tree by his window to sneak out in years. And when he had done it as a kid, it wasn't *actually* to sneak out, it was just as a fun game that he would play with his friends as they climbed around in the big trees that enveloped his back yard. This really was the first time that he had snuck out without his parent's knowledge. He was more shocked than anyone that he was contemplating it, let alone actually doing it.

As he got to the last few feet, he dropped to the ground from where he was hanging. As he did, he threw a look backwards and glanced inside his house. He froze in horror as his eyes locked directly onto his father's as he stood sipping from a coffee cup. Jason couldn't move at first. He did not hear anything of what Lou and Amy were saying. He just seemed frozen in place.

His dad's face never changed its expression as he brought the cup down from his mouth. His face was a stoic mask that betrayed no emotion. No anger, no disappointment. Nothing. He did, however, lift his coffee cup up just slightly as his head dipped in the direction of Jason as if making a toast. The actions were so slight in nature that Jason was not sure if he had just imagined it. But then, incredibly, his father casually turned and walked away from the window, never once pausing to look back.

1:17 PM, Monday, September 2nd, 1935

Just over seven hours prior to the Labor Day
Hurricane's Landfall

"So what's the goddamn problem?" The highly agitated foreman was not constraining himself any further as he screamed in to the phone at the East Coast Railway officials who were sitting dry and safe someplace in Miami, not about to get flattened by the worst weather that this particular man had ever experienced. "You get your goddamn workers off their asses, off the beach and on that rescue train before we get our rear-ends blown out to sea by this bitch!"

"Sir, if you would just calm down..." the rather droll and uninterested sounding official did not get to finish much of his bullshit answer.

"NO! I will NOT calm down. Get a crew together and get them down here immediately!"

"Sir, I am trying to explain to you that we are doing everything we can to get a rescue train down to you. The emergency locomotive #447 has not been steamed up yet, the crew hasn't been assembled yet and it is a holiday weekend *still*." Emphasizing the word would not have a good effect on the man on the other end, but the official really didn't seem to care much. "We are trying to get all of the cars hitched up and ready to move, but this is not a quick mission. Now," the official paused overly long as if giving the foreman time to regroup and calm himself down, "we hope to have the train on its way by 2 PM. That should give you plenty of time to load up your people and get far away from this whole mess."

The foreman pulled the phone away from his ear and stared at the phone as if it were a foreign object that he had never seen before. He slowly reached down to the desk and placed the receiver back into its cradle as he distantly heard the pompous official on the other end calling to him. "Hello...? Hello, sir? Are you..."

The foreman turned and stared down at the floor with an ashen look on his face, completely ignoring his compatriot in the small room. "So, damn you. Speak, man. What's the word? They coming for us or ain't they?"

The foreman slowly raised his face to look up at his friend as he fell backwards into the chair behind him. "They're leaving to get us by 2 today."

His friend's face brightened for a minute. "Well that's great news. If they leave by..."

"You idiot." The foreman spoke slowly, resolutely, as a man who had already seen the future and despaired for what was about to transpire. "They won't leave by 2! That trains' nowheres near ready to move. They won't leave by 3. Hell, we'll be lucky if they leave by 5 or 6. Or, if they come at all. When they miss their departure time by hours, they'll realize that we have no chance. They'll know its suicide. Even as strong and tough as these trains are, they need tracks to run on." He had lowered his eyes as he spoke, staring beyond the room they shared, but now he raised his eyes slowly again to his companion. "We're dead, boyo. You're just too dumb to know it yet."

Just over four and a half hours prior to the Labor Day Hurricane's Landfall

"So, where's the beach we're headed to anyhow?" Jason looked out the window at the gusting winds with trepidation. They had gotten out of the main city now and the streets looked like war zones. Tree limbs were everywhere. The limbs that were still attached bent and flowed in the wind this way and that like little twigs. The roads were masses of water, threatening to grab hold of their narrow car wheels and imprison them at any moment. He didn't want to appear scared in front of the others, but he was certainly having his doubts about the intelligence of what they were doing. Plus, his stomach and head were still in recovery mode and the swaying of the car in the strong winds did nothing to help make him feel any better.

"Screw that," Lou announced from the front seat. "I want to hear about how pissed your parents were. How bad did your dad skin you?

My bet was the belt with the buckle side out. Julie," he nodded with a smile to his girlfriend who looked absolutely terrified behind the wheel and never took her eyes off of the road, "thinks it was a switch. So… who won? Or was there a surprise implementation of torture."

Lou's eyes glinted with excitement, completely oblivious to the apocalypse that was occurring inches away from him just outside his window. He might as well already be on the beach with nothing but sunshine and butterflies, for all he seemed to acknowledge of their impending doom.

"First of all, are you blind?" Jason was almost yelling in order to be heard over the engine and the roar of the outside winds. He raised one hand and waved it around at the outside mayhem, as if showing Lou that they were stuck in the middle of a raging maelstrom would suddenly clue him into the precariousness of their predicament.

"And deaf?" Amy added in as she clutched Jason's arm even tighter, burying her face in his sleeve as yet another large crack of lightning lit up the sky.

Lou had almost been about to look away out the window following Jason's cue when he heard and saw Amy's reaction. Now he was focused back on Jason. With a "congratulatory" nod towards Amy, he gave Jason a big smile and a thumbs up. It was at this moment, that Jason realized that Lou really had no cares at all about what the weather was like.

Putting his other arm around Amy, Jason leaned back in his seat and scowled. In his mind, Jason could clearly see that this did not seem destined for a happy outcome.

3:33 PM, Monday, September 2nd, 1935

Just over four and a half hours prior to the Labor Day Hurricane's Landfall

Jason's mom placed the tray down on the coffee table and shook her head with a worried look on it. "Can you believe that there are fools out in this weather tonight? Going to get themselves killed is what they're going to do. And those poor tourists going back to the mainland on the train? Wouldn't catch me out on that thing tonight. I don't care whose wonder it is or what number wonder it is in the world. Mother nature is the number one wonder in this world and today is *not* the day to be messing with her."

His wife placed the tray on the table and then looked curiously over at her husband. "Are you ok, John? You haven't made a comment all afternoon."

"What's that?" His father stammered as he looked up at his beautiful wife. "A comment about what?" John tried to appear as if he was engaged in the conversation.

His wife now stopped with a stern look on her face and stood up straight with her hands on her hips, "Jonathan Henry, what's going on? What are you not telling me about? Is everything ok?"

John glanced nervously outside running his hand apprehensively through his hair, "Well..., I'm sure everything's fine," he started haltingly, "but, it's about Jason."

3:42 PM, Monday, September 2nd, 1935

Just over four and a half hours prior to the Labor Day Hurricane's Landfall

"Tom. What's the status? How much longer?"

Tom stopped pacing back and forth and scratched his head again. "They're not going to make it Mike. They say they're close... but..." Tom's voice was almost breaking as he spoke. "They aren't going to make it!"

"Tom." Mike spoke sternly but slowly again to his friend. "What's the status?"

Standing perfectly still now, all emotion and inflection removed from his voice, Tom whispered without ever looking at his boss. "They're hoping they can leave in the next hour."

Mike took the news in without saying a word. He stared at Tom for another moment before letting his gaze drop slowly to the ground. "I've doomed them." He stared morosely at the ground, the words settling slowly across the office. The workers in the room were starting to quiet down and turn their attention to him, as the realization that something terrible was happening swept like death across their ranks. They were not the ones however who were about to truly feel the terrible wrath of mother nature. But they were realizing that they were the ones who were going to have to deal with her aftermath. And the ones who were going to have to deal with the fact that they had failed their friends, family and loved ones who were on that train. "I've doomed them all." The words were barely a whisper now. He raised his eyes slowly to meet Tom's. "There's nothing more we can do now. There's nothing that anyone can do now. It's all my fault. I should have listened to you. I should have acted..."

Tom took a half step forward to his friend. "It was easy for me to make the call Mike. I wasn't the one in charge. I wasn't..."

"No!" Mike's word was strong and definitive now. He read it in Tom's eyes. The blame was no one's but his own. "You would have done what was necessary. I failed." He lowered his eyes again, unable to bear the reflection of truth in his friend's eyes. In any of their eyes. "No one is to blame for their deaths but me."

As the last words tumbled out of his mouth, one of the young ladies, Martha, in the back of the small room broke down into tears and fell into the arms of a co-worker. Mike jolted back to the present with the reaction. He looked up and started in her direction to help console her, but Tom moved a step into his path and shook his head solemnly.

Mike looked to his friend with the mannerisms of a soldier who's been shell-shocked from a compatriot's death. Dropping his eyes one more time in resignation, he turned and moved back to his desk. Sitting down without a word, he sat there silently for most of the remainder of the evening, knowing that he had not only doomed Martha's husband, son and two daughters to death on that train, but many others as well.

4:04 PM, Monday, September 2nd, 1935

Just over four hours prior to the Labor Day Hurricane's Landfall

"I don't understand." Grief was written all over his wife's face as she struggled to grasp the incomprehensible nature of the discussion. "You saw him leaving, knowing what's coming down on top of us and you didn't stop him? You actually encouraged him?!? You actually thought that this would help him in some way?"

"Well..." John stammered as he tried fruitlessly to come up with a way out of his current predicament. "I didn't actually say that I encouraged him..."

Now she was angry. "You *said*," she bit the word off as she annunciated it very clearly and slowly, "that you saw him leaving and that you let him go!"

"Well..." John drew the word out as he continued searching for his saving grace. "I did see him in the yard and leaving. But I didn't realize he was *leaving.* I thought they were just going to hang out in the neighborhood and goof off." He shrugged his shoulders and looked pitiful, as if suggesting that it was no big deal.

"Well..." Tricia did her best to control her temper as she flew around the house grabbing her galoshes, pulling her clothes on and grabbing her rain jacket and umbrella. "We do know they're gone now! Soooo... Get moving!!!"

"Huh?" He seemed confused by what was happening. "Ah, oh yeah. Yeah. I'm ready. Let's go get'em." Before he had even finished speaking, his wife had already pushed by him and was headed for the door. He ran to keep up with her as she slammed it open and barreled her way out into the storm.

4:40 PM, Monday, September 2nd, 1935

Just over three and half hours prior to the Labor Day Hurricane's Landfall

Tom hung up the phone quietly and turned to the huddled group who waited expectantly. "The train is on its way." A few faces brightened and started to smile. There was nothing jubilant in his face or his voice as he continued to speak the news. "They say they only left the station within the last ten minutes. They will make no stops between here and the Bonus Marchers and will be at maximum speed the whole way. No safety stops on the Keys. No looking for other survivors. They are only after the Bonus Marchers."

Martha spoke up. "And the Overseas Railroad?"

Tom looked up at her and shook his head. "They don't know. Maybe still in Key West. Maybe not..."

Martha tried to look strong this time and nodded as she lowered her eyes. She began to pray silently for her family. The woman next to her put her arm around her shoulders. No one spoke. All they could do now was wait.

5:00 PM, Monday, September 2nd, 1935

Just over three hours prior to the Labor Day
Hurricane's Landfall

The train rocked back and forth as the
winds buffeted the sides and the large rain drops
pounded on the side of the windows. Tina and
Sharon talked quietly as the little girl sat grumpily,
extremely bored now by sitting on the idle train
with nothing to do. She had lost all interest in the
crayons and paper. Occasionally she would kick
her tiny feet out at some imaginary target as an
outward expression of her anger, but these
demonstrations diminished as she realized that
the adults weren't paying her much attention.
Soon she was reduced to throwing her dolls and
other toys to the other side of their boxcar. Her
mother put a quick end to that behavior with a
rough slap of the young girl's hands. After a few
forced tears however, she went back to sitting
grumpily and making small grunts and whines of
displeasure.

Tina, greatly embarrassed by Patty's tirades and equally concerned about their predicament, nevertheless tried not to appear worried or upset for the benefit of her friend's daughter. And honestly for her friend's benefit as well. Having become a "society woman" seemed to have affected her friend in many ways. Tina knew the dangers of the weather they were facing, but Sharon seemed completely unphased by it. It was as if she considered herself exempt from the concerns of the common folk now. Tina knew that it would be bad though, once the reality of the situation set in with Sharon. In the meantime, however, Sharon appeared to look about her surroundings miffed and befuddled, as if she were beside herself with anger that the train had not already begun moving long ago. But Tina knew better. They would not be traveling today.

Not if these people knew their business about travel.

And not if they wanted to stay alive.

5:09 PM, Monday, September 2nd, 1935

Just over three hours prior to the Labor Day
Hurricane's Landfall

The perpetually sun-burned man in the little boat stared silently and stoically straight ahead at the darkening clouds. He was a seasoned sailor and was old and weathered. He had seen a thousand storms if he had seen one. He crinkled his brow slightly as he looked across the beautiful waters as they began to roil between him and the storm. Even as seasoned a sailor as he was though, it seemed as if the storm had literally just jumped from the waters before him to appear suddenly on the horizon, taking him completely by surprise. It was moving quickly. The pleasant, light rain that had gently dropped on him before was gone, replaced by a stinging rain that he knew all too well. The old man made the sign of the cross and then turned toward the direction of land as if to gauge the distance. Making the mental calculation in his head, he turned back to the storm and said a small prayer that appeared to be more along the lines of last rights, as opposed to asking for help. He slowly reached down and worked the small, reliable, yet sometimes touchy, engine until it finally sputtered to life. He began puttering, along making his way towards the distant, invisible land with a calmness that belied his impending doom. He was not an educated man, but his knowledge of the sea told him that this was effectively a futile effort. Life on the sea had been good to him, but he was fairly certain that his last day out here would not be.

5:12 PM, Monday, September 2nd, 1935

Three hours prior to the Labor Day Hurricane's Landfall

The conductor could barely be heard over the combined sounds of the train and the storm. He shouted as best he could, "What's the word, O'Leary?"

Shannon O'Leary was a beast of a man with fiery red hair that truly seemed to befit an Irish man of his size. But that was all that fit the stereo-type. O'Leary, as he was known to almost all, was as meek a man as you would ever meet. Shy around men and women alike, but extremely polite and likeable. He was the first to offer a seat to a lady and never one to get into a fight. He drank some pints back in the day according to his own words, but it wasn't much and he didn't like the way it made him. When pressed for what that meant, he would only describe it as "ornery". But when it came to taking care of his baby, steam engine number 447, no one was more particular or protective.

"We're turning around in Homestead, Cap."
The soaked fireman yelled back as he tended to
the boiler. Despite the howling wind gusts in
excess of well over 150 miles per hour, and the
rain pouring down on him as it flew horizontally
inside the exposed cabin, the lean, muscular
Irishman practically ran with sweat as he stoked
the fire. His muscles flexed mightily as he turned
back to his job digging his shovel head deep into
the mound of coal in front of him to heap more
fuel on the fire.

Normally, his fire lighters would have saved
him the grueling work by starting it up hours
before his arrival, but not today. Not on this time
table. They had already risked serious damage to
his beloved engine by firing it up so fast. It
normally required a substantial amount of time to
heat up slowly in order to protect the integrity of
the metal, but as he had rapidly fired up the
engines this afternoon, even as much as it pained
him, he knew that it was simply unavoidable.

The engineer, who hated that O'Leary
called him Cap, didn't need to do the calculations
in his head. It was already a little bit after 5 PM

and they hadn't even gotten to Homestead yet. This was bad. He yelled back at him. "We've no time to turn 'round in Homestead. We need to be makin' speed, not stops!"

A sudden gust of wind, and therefore rain as well, jumped up at them as they flew down the tracks. They both turned away from each other momentarily hands up in order to deflect most of the water before the Irishman could turn back to him and respond. "Not my call, Cap. They want us to be able to get out fast. You... people at... stop..."

Engineer Robert Walker could not make out anything else that his fireman yelled at him. Just random words that he was not even certain he heard correctly. The squall had blown up so bad on them at that moment that all talk was damn near impossible. Communication in general was cut off for the most part. The engineer stared at the back of the fireman as he had turned back to his work again and continued tirelessly to work the engine, trying to get more speed out of the beast. Robert knew that this was bad. He had been through plenty in his years with the railroad.

But this was something entirely different. This was bad... Really bad!

5:23 PM, Monday, September 2nd, 1935

Three hours prior to the Labor Day Hurricane's Landfall

"Where could they have gone?" Tricia gasped with grief. "Do you have any clue which direction they could have been heading? Anything that he said that could tip us off as to where they were going?"

John gripped the steering wheel tightly and continued to stare out through the windshield, leaning closer to it to get a better look through the rain and the utter darkness that was mostly shattered only by the large blasts of lightning ripping across the skies above. The raindrops streaming rapidly across the windows caused any exterior lights or flashes of lightning to shatter into splinters of wild visions causing him to continuously refocus his eyes. Still, despite the effort required to see where he was going, he wasn't sure if it was really an effort to try to see better, or just an effort to move further away from his wife's accusatory questions that was causing him to lean forward. She had already asked him the same questions 10 or 15 times. It did not matter how many times he told her that he did not know anything, she kept on asking him. Pounding into him over and over again the impossible nature of their predicament. The inescapable truth that they could not possibly succeed. It was her way of dealing with their powerlessness. Her only coping mechanism for keeping her sanity. Unfortunately, only a foot and a half away from her, staring straight ahead in a dejected manner with hunched shoulders, John had no way to deal with the helplessness. He had no coping mechanism other than to hide from her assault and hope against all hope that somehow, in some unknowable way, that through some miracle, they would find their son. But in the meantime, each question was a dagger into his heart that he had failed as a parent.

As if to emphasize the point again, she asked again after the moment of strained silence sat for too long. "John, are you even listening to me? How could they just disappear? They must have said something?!?"

Like a dog expecting the hit of a switch, he twitched and hunched his shoulders even further before turning slowly to look weakly at his wife. The words just stuck in his throat. He couldn't even think of anything to say.

Exhaling loudly again in exasperation, as she had done many times already that night, their car doggedly pushed on through the storm, the swollen streets continually grasping at the thin wheels, adding to the tension. Fortunately, it would be at least another five full minutes this time before she began grilling him again...

5:26 PM, Monday, September 2nd, 1935

Three hours prior to the Labor Day Hurricane's Landfall

After the rogue quartet of teens had snuck out of Jason's house, they had made a few stops for supplies on their way. One of the stops was at another friend's house, where they unsuccessfully tried to talk him into accompanying them. They hung out at his house for about an hour and threw darts for a little bit. Lou was extremely angry that his friend would not pick up his girlfriend and sneak out with them, but his friend kept insisting that the storm was going to be way worse than anyone thought. He implored the four of them not to continue on, but Lou was not even mildly swayed. He had visions of something incredible in his mind and he was simply not going to be dissuaded.

Moving on from there, another stop was to get beer from one of the small shops on the island where pretty much all of the underage kids went to get their liquor. Then they were finally moving across the heart of the island. Being that Key West is only 4 miles long, Jason didn't think it could have taken this long to get anywhere on the island. But with the added stops and how slowly the storm was making them travel, it was taking forever. Jason figured it had probably been about 5 hours since they had left his home and about 2 hours of that had been spent driving toward the far side of the island. Even though he had climbed down the tree around noon, and there had briefly been some sunlight through the clouds at that time, since then, it had been almost all darkness as they traveled making time stretch in Jason's mind. And amazingly, despite how long they had been gone, they were only now just getting close to the far side of the island where Lou was taking them.

Another part of the equation that was slowing them down was that the streets were already so far flooded that they couldn't travel on many of them. Although this was a common occurrence on the island, it didn't make it any less annoying. Or any less difficult to traverse.

They had to drive around the small dirt and paved airport to get to the farthest Eastern point of the island. Nothing was here except trees to the left of them and water to the right. As they approached the spot Lou was aiming for, trees appeared to their right as well.

The waves before they disappeared behind the trees gave the impression of being huge, massive even! And, they weren't constrained to the ocean either. The road was dangerously close to the sea at many points along US1, but it was apparently the only way to get to where Lou wanted to go. Wherever that was! Parts of the road were still not fully paved in this area and it made driving on the "road" even more treacherous. At one point a little more than an hour into the drive, Julie had become so terrified about staying on the road and dealing with the storm that Lou had had to switch places with her in order to convince her to keep going on. She didn't seem like she wanted to keep going forward regardless of who was driving, but they were absolutely not going to continue moving forward if she was the driver. And that was made abundantly clear to everyone in the car.

Amy leaned in close to Jason, placing her mouth directly against his ear before she spoke and cupped it with her hand to ensure that he was the only one that heard her. It didn't really make a difference though with all of the tremendous tumult of noise and mayhem around them, but she seemed scared to speak to him any other way. "I don't want to do this anymore."

Jason looked down at her. He nodded and tried to look comforting, but his words did her little good. "I don't either." Jason no longer cared if Lou heard him or not.

At that moment, Lou put on the brakes and stopped the car. They all felt it immediately. The sinking feeling! They had not been moving very quickly, and the road was already pulling at their tires, but now they could feel the car sink completely into the mud as soon as they stopped moving. No one mentioned it though. And Lou seemed not to care. He was looking around now, back and forth, craning his head this way and that, as if looking for something that should have been there. "Lost?" Jason ventured sarcastically, and in a voice that could not be described as anything other than bitterly angry.

Lou looked back over his shoulder as if just remembering that Jason was back there. "No worries." Lou shouted above the storm. "I'm sure we can get through over here." Lou gestured towards the side of the road off to the right of the car. Following Lou's signal, all three of his fellow passengers craned their heads that direction to see what on earth he was referring to. And all three of them quickly came to the same conclusion, Lou was nuts.

Jason didn't care anymore. He shouted at Lou, "You're insane. Not only do we *not* need to go that way," Jason wildly gestured with an angry expression to whatever Lou was looking at, "we need to get out of here, Lou. And we need to get out of here now! Turn this thing around. And do it right now!"

Jason waited momentarily for a response. When nothing seemed to be happening, he risked a look back to where Lou wanted to go. There was nothing over there other than more rain, more puddles, and more trees. But Lou saw

something that he wanted. Ignoring Jason, he
didn't even bother to respond. Instead, he put his
foot back onto the gas pedal again and he began
to drive the car... nowhere. The wheels spun and
spun without gaining any traction. The car didn't
even rock as the wheels moved. Terror was
written all over Julie's now ashen face as she
looked everywhere, from down at Lou's foot, to
back up to his face, to Jason and Amy in the back,
to outside the car and then back again to Lou. Up,
down, up, down, panic was mounting within her.
"Are... are we stuck?" Her voice was shrill and she
was sitting up higher in her seat now, gripping the
dash with one hand and the back of Lou's seat
with the other. "Lou? Lou? Are we stuck? Can
you get out? What's happening?" Words started
stumbling out of her mouth, some of them quickly
garbled up by the big bolt of lightning that
crashed what seemed to be right outside the front
window of the car.

"... down!" Lou was yelling. No one could
even hear the first part of his admonition for Julie
to regain her composure. The storm was
deafening now, and it was made even more so by
the rising fear that was welling in all of them now,

even Lou. Jason could see it. The fun and mischievous looks that had been playing all around Lou's face throughout their foolish expedition had finally vanished. Jason found no solace now in knowing that he had been right all along. They had no way of getting out of this ridiculous predicament that even a blind man could have easily foreseen. The car was stuck, and they had no way to free it.

Now the yelling began. All four of them spent the next few moments yelling at one another and screaming about what needed to be done next. Jason and Amy yelled at Lou for not listening to them. Julie yelled about how terrified she was. And Lou just sat in his seat hitting the steering wheel and cursing the car for not moving.

A slight lull in the pounding actually made Julie's strangely, suddenly subdued voice abruptly audible in the small enclosure. "The water!" She had turned back to the outside and now seemed mesmerized. The streets flooded all the time on the island, but this was something different. "What's happening?" Her voice was now so quiet. "What's happening with the water?"

The water had been momentarily receding from where it had gotten up pretty close to them, but they could see it building now in an odd way. It almost seemed to be rising up as if to strike, yet it was being held back at the same time by some invisible force. In an odd way, it was frighteningly fascinating to observe. Julie tilted her head just a little bit with her mouth hanging slightly open as she stared at the odd phenomenon.

But as quickly as the fascination had grabbed them, it turned even more suddenly into terror. It was not a twenty-foot wall of water, but it definitely was big enough to rock them. Lou was frantically trying to get the car to move again when the water slammed into the car with such ferociousness that it took them all by surprise. One minute it was standing tall, looking amazing and majestic, the next minute it was shattering glass and rocking the small vehicle up on to its two left side wheels. All of the occupants screamed at once, until only three of them were screaming. Lou had been slammed temple first against the side of the car and had crumpled silently into the door.

The car hung precariously on two wheels for just a moment as the water rushed by, until it could take it no more. One more big push of water was all it took. With Jason and Amy both pressed up against the far side of the car and Julie lying on top of her unconscious boyfriend, all of the weight had shifted. With a snap of the weak front wheel, the car buckled and then toppled all the way over on to its side. Fortunately, somehow or another, something grabbed hold of the car and stopped it from going all the way over onto the roof. Who knows if it settled down into the soft mud or if something blocked it, but regardless, they had thankfully stopped moving. Another foot or two more and they would have all been trapped in an inescapable, upside down watery grave. But not all of them were so lucky. Smothered by the press of Julie's body and completely limp, Lou's face went right down into the deadly mix of water, mud and broken glass. Julie fought frantically to lift his head, but the awkward nature of her body and the crazy positioning of being on their sides made her efforts fruitless. She screamed for Jason and Amy to help, but they were both busy fighting for their own lives.

Jason was trying to hold himself up from falling on top of and crushing Amy, much the same way that Julie had fallen on top of Lou. Splaying his legs and arms out in a vain attempt to stop himself, he did manage to lessen the blow of his weight upon her upper torso where he would have landed, if not for his desperate, flailing efforts.

Amy, for her part, was the one who had been the most prepared for the impending wave. For some reason, she had not been as completely transfixed as the others had been. She had been sliding away from Jason, and more importantly away from the anticipated impact. Because of her movement, she had not slammed as hard into the side door as Lou had and she had spared herself the same fate as had befallen her stricken classmate.

Jason looked down on Amy from above; his face held mere inches from her own, quivering with the strain of trying to brace himself from further pushing down upon her. Water streamed over his body from the broken window, formerly on the side of the car where he had been sitting. It came in intermittent sprays as other, smaller waves continued crashing over the upended, broken car.

Amy shook her head as she looked up at Jason. "We need to get out of here." She screamed at Jason as both continued trying to get their bodies into better positions to maneuver.

"I think I can get my foot onto the ground enough to be able to push myself out," Jason screamed back. Tension wracked his face as he struggled to dislodge his back foot and move it over her body. Amy closed her eyes tightly and stifled a grimace as more of Jason's weigh shifted on to her body. "There..." He moaned abruptly as he pressed down on his foot, before finally he screamed in pain. He knew immediately that his foot was broken or sprained. Not from any years of playing sports and dealing with sports related injuries, but more because he had to imagine that anything that hurt this bad, had to be a break. Or at least a very, very bad sprain.

Pushing up with a groan, he worked hard to extradite himself from Amy and lift himself into a semi-standing position, but instead he stopped half way through his motion. He looked over at Lou in the front seat for the first time since the wave had upended them. What he saw almost made him sick to his stomach. Julie was no longer trying to lift Lou's head. Only Lou's ear on the right side of his head was still visible. The rest of his face was hidden from view, engulfed entirely in mud and water. Instead of trying to fight any further, Amy's body had gone limp. She was still awkwardly situated with one hand lost from view in the mud and the other bracing herself by holding on to a portion of the steering wheel. Her head was bowed and she no longer fought to do anything. She had the look of a person who had given up. And indeed, she had.

Even though all of the water streaming over her head made it impossible for Jason to know if she was crying, he knew that she was. Her shoulders shuddered repeatedly as her tears dropped silently into the mud and water below. Jason grimaced as he stared at the horrifying scene in front of him. Lou was dead and there was nothing that they could do about it. Jason stared for one more moment at his friend's lifeless body. He had never seen a dead person like this before, up close and in his face. And definitely not someone that he had known so well.

He was still trying to figure out how to cope with this, when the car suddenly moved. Not a small movement, but a big, sudden movement that jolted them all back to the moment. Julie's head snapped up, her attention caught by the sudden panic again. The water was swirling around the partially submerged car and the continued movements of the currents and waves were still pushing the car this way and that as the water flowed back and forth. They were starting to lean again, on the verge of going over one more time and causing the car to end up on the roof. Sitting on their sides as they were, completely surrounded by water, if they rolled one more time, either back onto their wheels or upside down on to the roof, they would be entirely submerged at that point and would never have a chance. Sensing how much worse their position was about to get, Jason began yelling, "We have to move. We can't stay here. Get to your feet and look for a way out."

Jason was already doing just that, and now, so were the girls. Even Julie had been jolted back into action by the terrifying movement of the car. Both girls were looking up in the air shielding their faces as they tried to keep the rain from running unabated into their eyes. "I can't see anything," Amy yelled from below. "Jason, help me. Grab my hand." She was reaching blindly up for his grip, but he couldn't hear her, and he was already moving anyhow. Jason had gotten the far window, or what remained unbroken of it, unstuck and lowered. He was trying valiantly to lift himself from the watery prison that this car was soon to be for all of them, not just Lou.

Pulling up with his arms, he struggled against his own weight and the weight of his soaking clothes. Nevertheless, he was finally able to get his body up onto the outside of the door. From his momentary perch up there, he was able to survey the land. There was a building that they had not seen earlier a short distance away opposite of the way that Lou had been looking earlier to get them to the beach.

Looking back down into the car, Jason cupped his hands to his mouth and yelled. "There's a building that we may be able to get to. Give me your hands, so I can pull you out." Amy and Julie nodded in assent, miraculously both having heard him. Amy put her hands up first. After a short struggle, he was able to maneuver enough to get a good grasp on her hands so that he could pull. Although not an athlete, he was at least in decent enough shape for something of this nature. Jason was naturally strong in his upper body and he was able to lift her slowly up to the small window and pull her through so that she now sat opposite of him on the door frame.

"You have to make a run for the building, so I have room to get Julie out." The car shifted violently under them, falling back on its side as their weights shifted and the waters receded for a moment.

She shook her head vehemently. "There's no way I'm going out there without you."

Jason could tell that the terror in her eyes brooked no arguing. Relenting without another word of protest, he shook his head affirmatively and said, "but you have to move behind me, so I can get to her."

Amy shook her head and then tentatively moved on shaky hands and knees around Jason to the back of the car. From there, she collapsed shivering on the car and shut her eyes tightly not moving, trying to ignore the terrifying rocking of the car!

5:30 PM, Monday, September 2nd, 1935

Less than three hours prior to the Labor Day
Hurricane's Landfall

"Beer!" The prolonged and now extremely
uncomfortable silence between them was so
painful that it made it sound as if the sudden
outburst from John was a thunderous scream.

His wife jumped, startled even with the
pounding of the storm outside, by the suddenness
and the sharpness of her husband's outburst.
"What?!? Beer! What on earth are you talking
about, John?"

"Beer." He turned and looked at her
excitedly. "Think about it. What did we do when
we snuck out as kids? We got beer." John
pointed to the store up ahead as he turned his car
toward the front of the small store. "Wait here..."

Tricia did not bother to wait for the slow-
moving car to come to a complete stop. Having
caught onto his meaning, she was already jumping
out of the car and running through the rain to the

front door. John just sighed, bit back his unspoken words of restraint and moved the car into an empty parking spot on the side of the road.

Only one thing went through his mind over and over again as he put the car into park and leaned his forehead against the steering wheel. The same thing that had been going through it since this whole mess started. How could he have screwed this up so bad?

5:38 PM, Monday, September 2nd, 1935

Less than three hours prior to the Labor Day
Hurricane's Landfall

"The heart of the storm should be hitting us right now!" O'Leary was screaming every word just to be heard now. He could not even be sure that Walker was hearing him, but Robert was nodding in agreement.

"We don't have time for this!" Robert finally yelled back. O'Leary was sick of hearing Cap repeat this over and over by this point, but he couldn't argue with the wisdom of it either. The waves were now lapping at the rails according to some of the reports from up ahead. This was madness for sure now. There was no longer any point. If they went out over that water, they were dead men just as much as the men they were supposedly being sent to save. But O'Leary said nothing. It was not his place to question. Just to do.

Time just kept ticking away as they worked out the logistics of what they were doing. O'Leary knew from having been through these storms before that many people would never even consent to leaving their homes. They were used to just "riding out the winds." Nevertheless, here they sat in Homestead, waiting as the brain trusts figured out whether it would be better to have the light facing the rails on the way out, or on the way back. To O'Leary, time meant more to saving his life than any decision about the light. They weren't going to be able to see the tracks regardless with this darkness, these whipping winds and this God-awful slashing rain in their faces.

O'Leary was on the verge of telling Walker that they needed to just make a decision themselves without waiting and go, consequences be damned. They could just deal with the repercussions later. But even as he was still trying to drum up the courage to take this radical action that was way outside the norm of who O'Leary was, he picked his head up and looked out toward Robert as something caught the attention of his Cap. Immediately he saw Robert nod his head firmly one time in determined assent in the direction of someone or something that O'Leary could not see. Next thing he knew, Robert was waiving a finger in a circle above his head giving the sign to mount up. We're moving, O'Leary thought. Finally! The crux of the point that Robert was trying to get across with his hand signals was simply "Let's go!" And it worked. O'Leary felt the abrupt jerk of the train as it started to grind into motion again. They were moving slowly still as they were preparing now to turn the train around, so the light would in fact face backwards to make the escape quicker and easier. So much time had been wasted, but at least now they were off again. Somehow, to O'Leary, even though he now knew that he was headed to his inescapable death, this felt better than sitting on the tracks arguing. Moving always felt better than sitting to Shannon O'Leary. Especially with a category 5 hurricane staring him right square in the jaw.

5:51 PM, Monday, September 2nd, 1935

Less than three hours prior to the Labor Day Hurricane's Landfall

The old sun-burned man had been content when he had finally gone under. A small smile had played about his lips as he had fought his little engine, trying to keep the nose of his small boat pointed to where he thought land might have been located. He could not see a thing anywhere. As the rains slashed down upon his head and continued to push the nose in directions he didn't want it moving, he continued to smile and even tried whistling a tune over the howling of the winds. It was impossible. Even if he had been able to reach land, there was no way to see where he would land. He was so certain that he was close though.

The first wave that came all the way over the boat and his head, was also the one that nearly ended it all, before the fight had even really begun. But in the end, it wasn't enough. He was still alive. He was still fighting. Since that first wave in fact, he had fought for what felt like hours trying to outrun her. He had moved this way and that, trying to get out of her way, playing a man versus nature game of cat and mouse, but all along knowing that his would not be the last move to secure him victory. As the waves continued to crash over his head and the sides of his little boat, he thought back to his family. He had made mistakes in his life, but he had had his good moments too. Regardless of his missteps, in the end, he knew that he had always been a dedicated father, a kind grandfather, and as recently as a few months ago, a short-lived, but wonderful great-grandfather. The blessings of his life had been many.

His family thought that each time he went out, he went further and further out to sea, beyond where he should have gone, with the hopes that one day he would not return. They always joked with him that they would not be surprised when he didn't return one day, but that they would be sure to have a few beers and some pizza in his honor. He smiled broader as he thought about his friends sitting at his favorite beach side watering hole, drinking his favorite beer and eating the best pizza on the island. And they better be laughing he thought. He had always told them that he didn't want tears at his funeral. Just laughter and happy memories.

And honestly, there probably was a sliver of truth to the argument that it was his desire to pass at sea. He never envisioned himself laying in bed, fighting to breathe his last breath. Here though, as the waves continued to crash down upon him sapping the strength from his limbs, he enjoyed every minute of his struggle. As fervently as he fought to make one last heroic effort to get home, one last incredible story upon the high seas to impress his family and friends with, he also realized that he would be happy if this was the way the story was written. Fighting to live, and die, the way he had always wanted.

In his final moments, he never saw the decisive wave coming. The little boat that he had sailed for over 20 years with nary an accident, cracked with a loud snap that was not even a whisper due to the roar of the storm around him. As the back of the wave forcefully slammed his head into the hard side of the boat, throwing him unceremoniously into the water, the old man finally released his vice-like grip on the engine for the final time. No one would see his final moments. And he would never know that he had died within mere yards of safety. He had missed land a couple of times in his frantic race for survival, never knowing how close he truly was, but this time his limp, lifeless body found the sandy bottom of his new home.

He had faced the closing moments of his life with a smile on his face and an acceptance of what the ultimate result would be. The next victims of this storm, however, would not be such willing and understanding participants.

5:52 PM, Monday, September 2nd, 1935

Less than three hours prior to the Labor Day Hurricane's Landfall

"I'm sorry folks. There's been another delay. We're trying our best to get the train moving..." the hapless conductor did his best to sound reassuring and comforting, but it was to little avail.

"Screw that. We've been waiting for hours. We've been patient. We've heard your excuses and we're sick of it. When are we really leaving? I have to be at work in Miami tomorrow. Even if we left right now and experienced no other delays, I'd still not get home until 10 o'clock. This is not acceptable."

"Sir. Please understand. It is nothing that we can do anything about. It's simply too dangerous out there right now."

"I... don't... care!" The smartly dressed businessman who had already read his newspaper three times and looked at it a few more times without ever actually processing it, slapped it down onto his seat as he stood up to address the conductor. "I need to get home. NOW!"

The conductor had now already dealt with this situation many times before on this stalled take off, but this gentleman seemed the most agitated of any that he had faced so far. He stepped back a few paces and put his hands up in protest. "Sir, please understand. We have to ensure the safety of everyone on board. They have flat out told us, that we are not allowed to depart yet. They are saying that there are tracks out between here and Miami. Plus, more of them are blocked by falling debris. They even think that the water levels may rise to above the level of the tracks. This is not something that we can ignore. These are serious notifications and we cannot get trapped out on the tracks."

The businessman looked angrily around the railcar at the faces staring up at him and the conductor expectantly. The businessman's eyes locked with those of a young mother clutching her baby close to her bosom. Her face was clouded with fear and her eyes appeared wet from tears.

He looked down, angered and frustrated by the delays, but embarrassed by his disregard for everyone's safety. "Fine." He finally grumbled as he fell back into his chair, shoulders slumped. "I get it."

The conductor for his part, looked around the railcar, and not seeing any further challenges here, let his shoulders slump as he slowly moved forward, hopefully prepared to face the next angry passenger that he would surely find in the next car.

6:02 PM, Monday, September 2nd, 1935

Camp #5, Lower Matecumbe Key

Less than 2 hours and 20 minutes prior to

the Labor Day Hurricane's Landfall

Bill was sick of the smell that permeated every inch of the room. The stench of the room was the reek of sweat, panic and fear of the unknown. The storm had been battering their small, cramped headquarters for hours now. The phone had died long ago cutting them off from all communication and he was sick of everyone yelling stupid ideas at him.

They were in the worst possible defensive position imaginable for the unstoppable invasion of Mother Nature. She had them cornered. And even worse than being cornered, they were holed up in the lowest possible land on the small island. The position for Camp #5 may have been well thought out on Lower Matecumbe Key when the foe that they had been fighting was mosquitoes and the constantly burning rays of the sun. Now that they were fighting water though, not so good.

The fighting men who sat next to him shouting brainless suggestions were all well intentioned guys, they just weren't very bright guys. There was a reason that most of them had been grunts in the war. Sure, William Johnson, foreman of Camp #5 and triumphant hero of the Great War, was one of the rare exceptions. He was well read, a high school *and* college grad, and came from a wealthy family with lots of important business and political connections, but none of which were currently helping him in any way. He had done his best, but he had failed to get the mainland to move any faster in mobilizing the rescue train. His father's pull with the politicians a world away did nothing to move things along and now he had no suggestions about how to help save his comrades. Or himself.

A young man of twenty years of age when Bill had first jumped into the war, here he was now, nearly pushing 40 years old and he was completely devoid of any reasonable suggestions for a means of surviving the predicament they were currently facing. There were no easy answers. There was no terrifying foe to charge with bayonets raised. No rallying war cry that would help them to crush their enemies and win the day. There was only the hope that each of them could find a piece of earth to grab onto and ride out the storm while hoping their friends could do the same. There were no safe areas. No structures on the island were built to stand the pressure that was continuing to build. Bill had no idea how much stronger the winds would grow or how much higher the waters would rise, but at the moment, nothing showed any signs of lessening.

And so, they sat. Eight gruff, unhappy men. All tough as nails. All completely forgotten by society. All without any solutions. And they waited. And they listened. They listened to the intermittent screams of co-workers and friends as they were swept out to sea, or as they fought to hold on for their lives. Clinging to any piece of land, structure or tree that they could grasp hold of. None of them in that small, cramped room dared to attempt a rescue. Occasionally if a scream sounded extremely close by, they would risk looking out the small windows high up on the walls to see if there was in fact someone that they could aid. So far they had only been able to save Gramps as he came floating by nearly half dead. That had been early on in the afternoon as the flooding had just begun. He had been caught trying to get back to Camp #5 from the other side of the island. He said that another soldier who had just arrived two days earlier had gotten separated from him when a large wave had knocked them both over. The soldier was so new to the island in fact and had spoken with so few people, that no one, including Gramps, could even remember his name. Gramps had been lucky enough to get swept right up to the building in which they now sat, waiting for rescue or for disaster. They prayed for rescue but were prepared for the worst. At least for the moment, they were mostly dry and theoretically safer than the majority of the people on the island. If nothing else, they were saving up vital strength for when it would be their turn to have to grab onto something and pray.

They had eventually gotten sight of the fallen soldier, the 'new guy,' briefly about 15 minutes after they had pulled Gramps in. He was a good distance off and they had heard him yelling for help during a short lull in the early hours of the rains. Looking out the western window, they had quickly spotted him holding on to the top of a short palm tree. He had wedged himself in among the palms pretty securely. One leg was straddling the top of the palm in their direction, and the other leg was facing away from them. Periodically, the soldier would shift positions trying desperately to get a better hold onto the palms that kept slipping through his fingers.

They could see him alternately turning his head away from the waves and burying it into the crux of his arm to try to protect himself. After a moment or two, he would turn back around and try yelling out to anyone who might assist him.

The palm tree that he sat astride was his lifeline, but it also created problems for him. For one thing, it was one of the shorter palms on the island. And another problem was that it rested in a small indention in the land that made its total height even less than it would have otherwise been. The end result was that even though he was a total of about 17 feet above the ground directly below him, he was only two or three feet above the water for much of the time he was hanging on. This meant that every time a wave of any size came by, which was way too often, he got a face full of water. And sometimes his entire body was even submerged for short periods of time.

They had pondered for a short time the possibility of trying to reach him, but after the first few aborted attempts at a rescue, it was determined with much sorrow to be far too dangerous. The current and floating objects in the water made the idea simply too dangerous to contemplate any further. The next hour or so of listening to him scream for assistance had been agonizing. No one looked out the window at the abandoned soldier any longer as it was much too painful to see him hanging on for dear life, knowing that the outcome was never going to be in his favor. Listening to his cries for help that they could never hope to answer was almost as bad. In the end, they were never even certain when he finally washed away.

Gramps was the first to notice the lack of noise from the soldier for too long a time. Lifting his head from where it sat resting dejectedly in his hands, he paused for a moment and then turned to look at the western window. The storm still raged outside, but he could not hear the soldier any longer. Bill noticed his movement and looked up as well. Everyone now stared at the window, waiting. Hoping. His voice did not rise above the rains and winds again. After a moment, Bill slowly climbed to his feet and then stepped up onto the box beneath the window and from there onto the high table next to it in order to look out the window. His chin rested on the sill as he stood on his toes with his fingers grasping onto the sill and he stared out the window for a moment before letting himself fall back one foot at a time to the box first and then the ground below. He didn't say a word. No one needed to say a word. They just all silently bowed their heads and prayed for their fallen comrade.

That had been hours ago. Not much had changed since then. Except that eventually, the horrible ideas began again.

6:10 PM, Monday, September 2nd, 1935

2 hours and 10 minutes prior to the Labor Day Hurricane's Landfall

The amount of time that they had made up on the run was nothing short of amazing. The train seemed destined for the greatest run of its illustrious, yet often times maligned, career. O'Leary was truly beginning to believe that they might just have a chance to get out of this thing alive when the dream twisted back into a nightmare. A nightmare that had in fact never been erased, only obscured.

Many of the residents at stops along the way continued to refuse to board the rescue train, preferring instead to trust to God and their own devices. The stops though had taken a toll on their timing. O'Leary practically begged Robert to 'screw the orders from above' and just skip the remaining stops. Originally the plan had been straight in and straight out. What had caused the orders to change, O'Leary would never know. Nor would he care. All he knew was that this constant stopping was going to be the death of him. And of everyone they were attempting to rescue. Moving slowly from station to station and slowing down even more as they argued with people had really put them behind on their time table, despite the fast run of the train. Both Robert and O'Leary had argued before they left Homestead that just like had originally been decided, they should not make stops along the way given the reluctance of the people to leave and the lack of time for any errors. But that decision had been over-ridden by someone higher up at the last minute. And now there was no longer any way to ignore the decision without just flat out ignoring it. A thought that had been considered multiple times by both men, but not one that Robert, who was ultimately responsible for the train, was willing to act upon. At least not up to this point anyhow.

Now came the harshest blow of all however. Just as they were slowing down and beginning to move into the train station at Snake Creek they had to slam on the brakes. The Cap was witness to an awesome sight. One he wished he had never had the sore misfortune of getting to see.

A huge gust of wind had blown up moments before the great train was set to glide into the small station, which was honestly not much more than a block of cement for loading and unloading. The gust of wind did what it had been setting up for hours, ripping an electrical wire loose from its moorings and thrashing it about on the tracks in front of them with deadly force, like a vicious, venomous snake. The sparks jumped and skipped about in the rain and wind, setting up an amazing light show on the tracks that just about made both grown men cry. They were forced to stop the train short of the platform and set about fixing the wire from there. The loose cable would eventually end up costing the rescue workers a full hour before all was said and done. One hour ripped from their trip in a race against time. One hour that could not be afforded. One hour that they had no capacity to avoid. One hour that might end up costing them all of their lives that night.

6:10 PM, Monday, September 2nd, 1935

2 hours and 10 minutes prior to the Labor Day Hurricane's Landfall

Amy lay shivering at the back of the car with the cold metal pressing against her face, not daring to move. The front of the car had shifted forward now, so that she was at the apex of the back-right corner as it was thrust higher into the pouring rain. The large, cold drops of rain were pelting her now with an even greater intensity than previously, stinging her skin painfully with each drop. The wind had dropped in intensity, which seemed odd, because the intensity of the waves had not been reduced at all. The waves just kept coming at them with no visible end in sight. In fact, she couldn't even force herself to lift her head to look out towards the ocean at this point to see if there was an end in sight. She feared for what awful vision might assault her senses next if she turned to look. She had never been so scared in all of her life. Almost too petrified to move, she couldn't even think coherently enough to pray for salvation. All she could do was hold on and shiver.

Even worse, not able to see what was happening in the car below, she couldn't understand how it was taking so long for Jason to get Julie out of the car. All that was visible to her was the bottom half of his body as he leaned back into the car to reach her. Julie must not have been willing or able to move at first however, as she could just barely hear Jason, but he was definitely yelling at her. On top of that, she could see his body moving about on top of the car constantly trying to get a better position from which to try to haul her out.

And, even though it felt like it took an eternity before he was able to finally succeed in coaxing her out of the wreckage, at least he was eventually successful. Which meant that they could then finally try to move too. Amy did not want to spend another second exposed on the top of the car. Unfortunately, although Julie was now out of the car, it also took time to create enough courage within her to convince her to make an attempt for the building. The water swirled all around them and all three of them knew that they could never stay on top of that car and live, but they couldn't get Julie to stop staring at Lou. She just kept crying and mumbling words that neither of them could hear nor understand.

Finally though, Jason had seemed to get through to her. Amy was going to be the first to go across. Jason convinced her that Julie had to see that it was possible, or she would never try. And he couldn't go first because Julie went absolutely berserk shrieking at the top of her lungs the moment he had let go of her hand saying that he was going to leave.

Jason turned and looked at Amy. He shouted at her, "We need you to do this Amy. If we stay here any longer, we are going to..." He broke off what he was saying and looked back anxiously at Julie, although if she had heard anything he had said, she gave no indication of having heard him. Or, of caring. Despite that, he continued speaking in a more guarded manner as he looked back at Amy, "We just cannot stay here. It's only going to get worse." Amy finally lifted her head and managed a weak nod. Her strength was rapidly flowing from her body. She felt more exhausted by the minute. Her desire to move from this spot was quickly being replaced with a desire to just lay here with her cheek pressed against the solid, cold reassurance of the metal bumper. Her mind knew that she couldn't remain where she was, but her will was beginning to desert her.

Jason looked hastily over each shoulder, his mind working hard to find the best way out of their clearly dire predicament. He could only come up with one viable means of them making it to safety. Settling on what he saw as his only chance for survival, he turned back to Amy with a determination that brooked no further disagreement. "Listen to me," he grabbed her shoulders and helped to lift, almost drag her to her knees. "We have no choice. You have to do *exactly* what I tell you." It wasn't that what he was telling her was so complicated; it was more that he needed her to focus and get prepared for what she needed to do.

Just as he barked the last word, a huge wave suddenly crashed into the car, shifting it violently to the side. All three of them gasped and yelled as they frantically scrambled to rearrange their grips in order not to be thrown into the swirling waters below. Jason froze for a moment, trying to push down the unexpected and sudden panic. As the spasm of fear passed, he regained his composure and locked eyes with Amy again. To his surprise, this time he was the one who had remained panicked the longest between the two of them. She was already looking at him, calmly now, awaiting his orders. The look of confusion must have been evident on his face. She yelled dispassionately at him in response to the unspoken question in a flat tone, "I want out of here. *Now*!!!"

Jason nodded. Looking back over Amy's shoulder for a moment to reassess the situation, for some reason, he actually felt now like maybe they had a chance. "Alright," he looked back to her, "I am going to help you stand up and steady yourself. You are going to have to launch yourself as far as you possibly can." He paused for a second to give her a chance to nod affirmatively. This time they didn't even blink as the car shifted under them. It was slightly less of a shift under them this time, but still, it was definitely a shift and they should have been shaken by it. But they weren't. They were just so much more dialed in and focused at this point that it just didn't register nearly as much this time. He pressed on, "You need to immediately begin attacking the water. Don't look around, don't look back, no matter what you do, no matter what you hear. You have to get to that building. See if you can get inside. Maybe you can find something to help us. A phone, rope, anything useful. But then, get back outside as soon as possible. You need to try to catch Julie if she doesn't make it all the way across."

Amy took a deep breath, "What if…"

Jason didn't even hesitate, "You're going to make it!" Shaking his head affirmatively, he waited for her to do the same. She shut her eyes as her head bobbed up and down to show she agreed. He wasn't sure whether she actually believed it or not, but it no longer mattered. Time was running out. Squeezing her shoulders, he helped to push her up into a squatting position on her hands and feet facing slightly away from his body and toward the building now. "Focus." Her body shook, but she responded.

Looking back momentarily at the crashing waves as they kept coming at them relentlessly, Jason tried to time it up properly. He physically nodded his head slowly as he tried to mentally judge for himself when the best time to launch her would be. He wanted to push her off into a wave as if she were body surfing, but he was not certain if the wave would crash in on her and simply smash her into the ground. He decided in the end that it would be better if she was already swimming and was out away from the overturned car when she dealt with the crash of the water. Maybe she could get under it before it came down upon her.

Still judging the distance, he thought that maybe he saw his opening. He moved closer to her and crouched as she had with his body next to her. One hand was on her upper arm and the other was on her waist, so he would have what he hoped was the best possible grip for propelling her forward. He repositioned his hands once or twice on her trying nervously to get the best grip.

"Get ready," he yelled, never taking his eyes off of the wave, but he could feel her nodding affirmatively as she continued to gin up her own confidence. "Take the brunt of this wave, and then we're going to jump up and go! Be ready..." The wave hit with a lot of force this time. The car buckled a lot but did not shift further. Jason had waited for a particularly large wave as he figured maybe the waves after this big one might be smaller as she swam. His hopes sank. Even as they both jumped up, trying to shake the water from their eyes, he immediately knew that he had miscalculated. The next wave looked every bit as big, if not bigger than this one. There was no time to change the plans though. Amy had already prepared herself and they were both moving. He didn't want to make her anymore nervous, or worse, try to stop her from jumping and have her fall off the car awkwardly before she could stop her momentum.

With a great heave of all the energy he had left, Jason put everything he could into pushing Amy out away from the destroyed vehicle. Amy pushed into the jump with everything that she had left and actually connected very well with the water. Arms outstretched, she sliced perfectly into the water. Even as she broke the water though, she knew that something was wrong. She had felt it in the way Jason had released her. Her heart dropped. Jason had slipped as he had propelled her off the car. She just knew it.

As soon as she emerged from the raging waters, she did exactly what he had told her not to do. She couldn't help it, she had to see if he was ok. As much as the water was roiling angrily around her however, she could not even make out his silhouette. Then her heart sank as it suddenly dawned on her why she could not see him. A wall of water was rising in front of her. All thoughts of Jason were erased from her mind as her body's instinct for self-survival kicked in massively. Turning toward the building, she could not even take one stroke toward the building as the shock of it hit her. She was already there! The strong undercurrent must have pushed her way farther and faster than she even realized as she had propelled herself from the car. The building was a mere ten feet in front of her. She must have flown underwater to have moved so far, so fast!

As she looked back and found the wave about to pound down on top of her, she quickly understood her most imminent danger. The good news is that she had shot straight as an arrow towards the shed. The bad news though, was that if she went any further forward like she did when she leapt from the car, she was going to smash headlong into the building and probably break every one of her vertebrae, and even if she didn't, she definitely would knock herself unconscious.

Putting her head down first, she tried to dive for the ground. Based on the height of the building still showing above the water and the fact that her feet were not touching here, it seemed as if she still had a lot of room to dive. And she did. She must have been on sloping ground or in a ditch, because she was able to kick down reasonably far before making contact with her hands on the moist land below. Debris slashed at her body as it flew rapidly by her in all directions. She felt the massive wave above her grab her body and toss her effortlessly back and forth. Her fingers scrabbled along the ground trying to grab any kind of purchase to hold onto. At first there was nothing. She had only been a small distance from the building when she had gone under just a few seconds ago. As her body moved from where it was floating vertically and her feet starting dragging her horizontally away from where she was, she knew she did not have much time to find herself an anchor before the buildings walls, or anything else that might be under here, met her body in a very unhappy manner.

Her fingers dragged desperately across the land with no success for what seemed like an impossibly long time without end, but what was probably only five to ten feet. This left her only a few remaining. Panic was welling up in her as she started to brace for the inevitable impact when she finally got it. There it was, her lifeline. Grabbing on with all her strength, she squeezed tightly. Something was there on the ground, she never even knew what it was that saved her life, but she held on desperately as the wave continued to pass over her.

Her lungs were burning when she finally felt secure enough to let go and push for the surface. As she did, the water automatically pushed her even closer towards the building. As she broke the surface, she was clearly in much shallower water here as she popped well out of the water with her head at least two feet above the water with her feet planted on what felt now like cement below. And she was now no more than a foot away from the left side of the building. Getting her feet securely underneath her body and pressing her back thankfully against the solid, reassuring feel of the buildings wall, she realized that she was only in about three feet of water now while it was down between waves. She was sure more waves would be coming, but for the moment it was fairly near to the ground. She let her chin drop for a minute as a feeling of relief washed over her. The water continued to swirl around her waist, causing her body to sway back and forth. She looked up suddenly, snapping back into the moment and realizing that she did not have much time before another wave came crashing down on top of her. Turning her head quickly to the left and right, her brain swiftly registered that she was much closer if she moved to her left. She looked towards the car for a moment and struggled to see something, anything on the car between the waves and the rain coming down.

Nothing. She could barely make out the silhouette of the car, but where they were on the car, she couldn't tell. Her mouth opened in a silent scream as she saw a wall of water rise up in front of her so swiftly that it seemed as if it appeared from thin air. Turning to run the five steps to the left to get around the wall to move to the far side, she only made it two slow wading steps around the corner when something solid slammed into her back, knocking her forward on to her hands and causing her to gulp down a significant amount of putrid water.

Spluttering and struggling to catch her balance and get back up, she initially thought the wave had hit her sooner than expected. As the pair of arms reached around her waist and she felt the substantial body press against her from behind, she realized that Jason had made it across. And smashed right into her.

Looking awkwardly over her shoulder they both continued stumbling towards the back side of the building. She heard his desperate voice gasping out to her as he coughed up and spit out water, "Keep moving. It's coming."

She didn't need to look back this time to know what he was talking about. The building was slender, which offered them hope, but even so, their progress just seemed so painstakingly slow. Stumbling and falling, Amy reached out and grabbed the corner of the building as larger and larger waves began pounding against her back.

As they both wearily lunged around the building for the safety of its bulk, and before she could even let the relief of their success hit her, her heart rent in half. "Am-..." She heard and saw Julie at the same time. Amy's face was twisted in grief and anguish. She never even saw her friend's face before Julie was swept back under and away. Amy heard her gargled voice start to call to her, and then for a brief moment she saw Julie's upraised hand reaching out for her friend in desperation before it was pulled back under once more and hidden from sight.

Amy started to rise to try to move in her direction, but Jason tightened the grip on her waist before she managed to move forward and held her back. Looking back at him in shock, no words coming from her mouth, Jason shook his head negatively. "It can't be done." He emphasized the word can't in a monotone manner. It was a manner that suggested how much it hurt him to say the words, yet conveyed the meaning that his warning was not to be ignored.

Tears flowed from her eyes as she let her body slump in defeat back onto Jason's body and the wall behind her. Her head popped up momentarily in expectation. She swore that she heard Julie's faint voice one more time, but far away and tiny. She could see it in Jason's face as well. He had heard it too. But neither of them moved. There was no point. Now, she really was gone!

7:22 PM, Monday, September 2nd, 1935

Less than 1 hour prior to the Labor Day
Hurricane's Landfall

"More than an hour lost, Cap!" O'Leary
continued shouting at him as he had been the
whole trip. "Now, we still have twenty more
minutes to get to the camp." O'Leary looked
away for a moment trying to get the water and
sweat from his eyes, but also trying to will the
exhaustion from his mind and body. "We can't do
it, Captain. It's too much. We need to turn
around now and make for the mainland. We
might still have a chance if..."

Robert cut him off before he could go any
further, "Shannon." Cap never called him
Shannon unless it was something extremely
important. And nothing was ever that important
with Cap. "We aren't leaving them out there." He
paused for a moment, and then went on, "None
of them!"

O'Leary stared him in the eye for a long
moment, before he nodded one time with a stiff

movement of his head. If Robert Walker was going all the way, you damn well better believe that Shannon O'Leary was going to go with him. "Aye Cap. All the way it is." Without another word, O'Leary turned around and began working the big bellowing engine again.

Who knew, he thought wryly, maybe they could still do it.

7:25 PM, Monday, September 2ⁿᵈ, 1935

55 minutes prior to the Labor Day Hurricane's Landfall

"Maybe we missed something." Amy spoke quietly, despite the loud pounding of the storm outside. She sat with Jason's protective arm draped around her shoulders sliding up and down her bare skin trying his best to keep her warm. Her shivering had lessened now, but she was still noticeably cold and wet.

"We didn't miss anything," Jason answered back quietly. "I've looked three times. There's nothing here."

She glanced around the mostly unlit room. There was a lot of electronics in the room, as well as some janitorial supplies. It was obviously some type of communications hub or emergency generator for the airport, but it did not appear that it was getting a whole lot of use anymore. Even prior to the storm, it looked like the place had taken a beating. What was probably years of little, to no, use, had left the place looking deserted and rotted. There was communication equipment evident in the form of radios and such for air traffic control, but none of it was functional according to Jason. He had limped around the damp, depressing room wading through the foot or two of standing water a few times trying to get something to turn on. Amy had sat there shivering, refusing even to move around. She preferred to just stay where she was with a solid, cement wall at her back.

Water swirled gently around them when he finally took a seat, eventually even rising over their ankles and soaking their bottoms. Amy never acknowledged it though and Jason didn't want to move. She had calmed down some now. He had no desire to disturb her any further than he needed. He however felt very uncomfortable sitting in the dirty water. He could only imagine what was floating around in the black, murky water. Probably lots of bugs, dirt and God only knew what else. He tried to keep the look of disgust off of his face when she looked at him, but again, Jason didn't think that she even really saw him when she looked in his direction. Amy was so absorbed with what was going on inside of her own mind, that Jason was a mere after-thought at this point.

"So, then what do we do now?" It had been a while that they had been sitting there not saying anything, staring at nothing in particular, when Amy finally voiced the question that they were both thinking. Perhaps Jason was too much of a man to ask the question, but she wasn't afraid to ask it. They were alone, scared, cold, hungry, wet and no one would have any idea where they were at. They hadn't told anyone where they were going except for the guy at the corner shop where they had bought their beer. And no one would ever think to ask that guy. Plus, he would never remember a couple of idiot kids babbling on to him about heading out to the beach just on the other side of the airport. And they didn't make it there anyhow. How would anyone even think to find them over here even if they did find the overturned car. She assumed that it would make sense for them to seek shelter in here, but that still required someone finding their car in the first place. Which led back to the original problem of no one knowing that they were out there.

Amy kept running over it again and again in her mind to see if anyone would be able to piece together where they had gotten too. When would they even figure out they were missing? At some point while her and Jason were whispering to each other in the back of the car, back when their little adventure had been fun and mischievous, not foolhardy and deadly, back when Lou and...

She stopped herself. It was too soon. She couldn't even think about them without starting to cry. Jason looked at her as he noticed a sudden change in her posture. She looked up at him with the tears starting to form, her shoulders gently heaving up and down as she shuddered. As he looked into her eyes, he didn't have much strength left inside himself to offer her much solace. He pulled her in tighter and gave her a kiss on the top of her head. It was mostly so he would not have to answer any of the questions or the pain that he was reading in her thoughts, but he told himself it was for her. He was consoling her, not being a coward.

Back to her thoughts as she put her head down again, almost oblivious to his small show of compassion and understanding, she thought back to those more pleasant, fleeting moments in the car again. She remembered something that Jason had said to her while they were still smiling and having fun. Before the storm had started to worsen and scare them. Before all of it. Something that was very odd. He had said that he thought his father had almost saluted him as he had "snuck" out the backyard. He was positive that his dad had seen him, of that he was certain. But what he couldn't figure out, was why his dad had saluted him. He was almost certain that his dad had been proud that Jason was actually defying him for once. She remembered that Jason had been truly baffled by the whole situation.

At the time, all she remembered thinking was, 'how awesome is that? Your parents don't mind that you're sneaking out.' Now all she could think was, 'did his father know where they were heading? Would he chase after them? Would he have any idea where to go?'

Finally, Jason spoke, softly moving his arm once again on hers in a gentle motion, still trying to keep her warm. "I don't..."

"Shhhh!" Amy stiffened and sat upright, pushing his arm partially away in the process. Now they both sat perfectly still waiting to see if the sound came again. "I think someone's out there." Amy's voice now rose in volume as she got excited.

"It has to be Julie. She must have found some way to..." Her voice was cut short by another sound. Someone was now right up against the door and making a lot of noise as if they were trying to get inside. "JULIE! JULIE!!!" Amy was screaming now as she jumped up and ran to the door. "JULIE!" Her voice rose even higher now as someone was clearly pulling desperately on the doors trying to get them open. Something was unquestionably blocking their efforts though. "JASON!!! Jason, come help. Please. We need to get Julie. We need to help her!"

Jason jumped up awkwardly, using both hands to push himself up off of the floor, in order to alleviate as much pressure as possible from his swollen ankle. He began hobbling his way over to the door as quickly as his injured foot would allow him in an effort to help open it up. But even as he moved to the other side of the building, he knew who he would find on the other side of the doors. Or more precisely, who they would not find on the other side of the doors.

First of all, there was no way Julie could have been able to clear that water without someone's help. Second of all, she had already been exhausted when they had still been on the top of the car. After the swim, she would have had no energy left for anything. And finally, and worst of all, Jason had seen her. He saw the look in her face. He knew she had given up. She had almost given up entirely when she saw Lou. She had almost given up when they were laying on top of the car being hit non-stop by the waves and knocked this way and that. And she had definitely given up when Jason had let go of her. He would never be able to forget that look on her face; the look of betrayal. He knew it would haunt him for the rest of his life.

Jason had slipped when he had tried to help propel Amy off of the car, just like Amy had thought. He had put too much pressure on his injured ankle and it had buckled under the strain causing Jason to slip off of the side of the car just as Amy had jumped into the water. His foot and leg had plunged straight down into the water and stretched his groin painfully as his other leg remained securely on the side of the car jammed against the door handle. Momentarily forgetting her fear, or terrified of being left alone on the car, or just plain reflexively, Jason would never know which, Julie had slid across the car on her belly to grab Jason's arm. Unfortunately, she was not securely holding on herself as she tried to pull him back up. Instead of being his savior, she actually ended up pushing him further off the car.

Now he had no way of getting back up. His other leg was ripped off of the car as well and Julie came down in a disorganized tumble right behind him.

When she hit the water, Jason was right next to her trying to help her, but she almost pulled him down with her she was in such a panic again. All thoughts of trying to help Jason had vanished the minute her body touched the water. She instantly reacted like a drowned rat, scratching, flailing around and trying to get back onto the car. She had a hold of the car for a moment before Jason lost sight of her. A wave came up at that moment, the much larger one that had chased after the one he had thrown Julie into, and smacking him square in the face, it sent him straight down to the bottom, which at that moment was not very far away. This was a good news, bad news scenario for them. Being as shallow as the width of their car, the good news was that it would have allowed Jason to stand up and have his head out of the water. But, the bad news was that being as shallow as it was, it also allowed the huge wave that hit him to crush him back-side first into the ground before he could recover to stand. After finally getting his feet under himself however, he managed to push up and break the surface of the water again for a second. He had not even been able to get himself steady in the swirling water though, when Julie came crashing into his side. Grabbing on once more, they were quickly swept away from the car and pushed out into deeper water and toward the building where Jason fervently hoped that Amy anxiously waited for them.

As they got pushed further away from the car, the ground continued to slope down, making it more difficult for Jason to find purchase on the unseen ground below. He was still trying to get his bearings to see which direction they should be heading in order to reach the building. Amy, however, was in total panic mode. Even though she was relatively tall for a girl her age, she still never would have been able to stand up in the swirling water. Her panic kept her from behaving in a rational manner that would allow her to get her feet planted. Instead, she continued to flail around wildly, her eyes large and her mouth open wide as she screamed insanely. The only time she did not scream was when the salty, dirty water poured into her mouth causing her to gag and choke. And this only served to increase her panic further and made calming her down completely impossible.

At first, he had tried to fight her. He had screamed at her to listen or to stop yelling. He fought with her to try to get her upright and oriented, but none of it made a difference. She was too far gone to let him help her. All she did was continue to make things worse by the moment. Eventually he had to make a choice. It was him or no one. He knew that neither of them would make it out of that swirling, watery coffin if he stayed with her.

The shame that Jason would never be able to live with was the fact that he had to consciously decide to kick away from Julie to avoid being pulled under with her. As he disengaged himself from her, he did not intentionally push her or pry her fingers from him, but as she was swept away from him with no will to resist, he made no effort to reach out to grab her. He watched as she looked back at him for a moment before going under. He saw it in her eyes. She knew that he had purposely not tried to pull her back. She knew that she could not be saved, but all he saw in her eyes was the accusation that he would not even try.

And worst of all, the shock of seeing Jason let her go, actually caused her to forget her panic for a moment. Julie stopped shrieking as she floated rapidly away, causing Jason to momentarily move to save her when he realized what had happened, but he was nowhere near fast enough to recover. Julie was moving so fast now, that she was gone before he knew it.

The shame burned inside of him now as he stumbled to within a few steps of Amy's side to try to help with the door. Knowing that Julie would not be there to judge him again with that look, but dreading that she might be by some incredible miracle, and the fact that he dreaded the miniscule chance of her remarkable deliverance, made him hate himself even more.

The crashing on the door got even louder as it was pulled outward a good four to five inches before slamming shut again with a significantly large bang. Jason pulled Amy back from the door before it slammed shut. He was scared that in her unbridled excitement to find Julie that she would get her hands or fingers caught in the door as it slammed shut. Better to wait for whoever was trying to free them to be successful on their side than to risk getting hurt on theirs. The force of the water on the outside of the door gave it the force of a hammer on an anvil as it crashed back into place. Water had poured in through the door the second the opening in the door was created.

Now that the door had slammed shut again, it slowed abruptly to a tiny trickle. Amy stopped, stunned for a moment and stared at the forbidding door once more.

They could hear excited chatter from outside as at least two, maybe three people discussed something anxiously. Then they heard a final affirmative answer before silence again. After a few more moments, they heard the door start to groan again. But this time as it started to open, a large metal pipe was thrust in through the doorway temporarily propping it open. Water flowed now nonstop through the opening into their temporary, mini-fortress. A moment later the water increased as the door continued to open further. Amy could see, and now hear, as someone was leaning into the metal poll pushing on it to get better leverage. The more the door opened, the faster it seemed to move, and the less resistance seemed to be given by the water.

Next a hand came through and then a shoulder. Amy and Jason were now frozen, feeling the increase of the water's tide on their feet as more flowed in, just watching as the door was finally pushed ajar. All thoughts of helping whoever was prying open the door had long been forgotten as they waited with open mouths. Finally, it was open.

Julie was not there. It was a man, a janitor in fact, judging by his soaked uniform. Standing there gaping at them with his foot now wedged at the bottom of the door and his shoulder pressed against the middle, forcing it to remain open despite the pressure of the running water. The small maintenance building was already filling with water. It was quickly knee deep, and then even faster it moved higher than that.

"I said, are you two ok?" The man apparently had been speaking to them.

"Come on Tally, give 'em a little room now. They must be scared to death." The woman behind the man that she had called Tally, was trying to shoo him out of the way.

"You the people they all bin' looking for back in the city proper?" Tally was squinting like he might recognize them.

"Tally, damn you. I said, git out of the way you big hulk. Now git! These kids need to get someplace warm and safe." Now the woman was really trying to swat the man on the back and arms to encourage him to move. Looking at Tally, Amy really couldn't see how the man could be called a "hulk". He was built more like a twig, than any kind of a muscle man. The tall, lanky guy almost seemed to be "slow" working on the mental side. He seemed kind of dim as he slowly reacted to the determined woman's prodding's. Shifting out of the way, they got a look at who stood behind him. And then at that point, what she really didn't understand was how this plump, little woman behind him had been able to survive out in this storm for more than five minutes. While the "hulk" stood at about 6'3 and 190 pounds of nothing but skin and bones it seemed, the woman behind him couldn't have gotten to much more than 5 feet, if that. And she was on the stockier side it appeared.

Almost as if reading her thoughts, Shelby intoned cheerily, "Trust me, I do ok for myself when the shit goes down out here." Shelby smiled a weary smile. "Pardon my French. Now, how about we try to get you two inside..."

7:58 PM, Monday, September 2nd, 1935

22 minutes prior to the Labor Day Hurricane's Landfall

"CAPTAIN!!! We... are... out... of... time!" O'Leary was shouting. The barometer had fallen so far below anything he had ever even heard of before that he was certain it was no longer working. "We need to..." O'Leary practically fell off of his feet as he ducked down in the train from the huge wash of rain from the sudden gust. Pulling himself back up, he finished yelling, "Go!"

Robert was practically sitting down at the front of the train, struggling to get to his feet and start the train moving forward. Every thought and every action right now demanded all of his attention just to complete it. He had been awake for fourteen hours now, with his nerves being stretched every minute of the last nine hours almost as much as the strength of his sinewy arms. He felt like he had not slept or rested in days. No stranger to hard work himself, Robert considered himself to be in tip-top shape for a man of his age. He was proud of his physique and worked hard to maintain it. But at this moment in time, all he could think about was how tired and cold he was. Forcing himself to get back on his feet, he raised himself up again to where he could try to see the tracks in front of the train. Failing that, he simply tried to get the train moving again. As it slowly lurched forward this time, it no longer seemed like the great force of nature that it had once appeared to be. Instead, now it seemed tiny and insignificant in the face of the truly awesome and magnificent force of Mother Nature which now pounded against them mercilessly. The train seemed to disappear into the night as it moved slowly out of the station. Minutes ticked by as they slowly proceeded down the tracks. Having turned the engine around earlier in the night at Homestead, Robert was trying to use this advantage to see what was in front of him. The light was of just about no use though. The only images to show up within its feeble glow, were the sheets of rain and wind that were pounding down upon them with such force and fury as to make the whole world vanish in a haze of darkness, dread and distress.

They were ten minutes from the station at Lower Matecumbe when the first wave really hit them. The screams of terror from the mostly male soldiers had started to rise now. Blooded men, who had seen visions of war in Europe that made the most seasoned soldier cry, screamed now in terror as the train was buffeted side to side. The few women and children on board who had not gotten off at the last stop had already begun to cry and call out much earlier. A few people at the last stop however, had decided that this train had taken them far enough and that solid land was the better option for their best chance at survival.

After the second wave hit a few moments after that, to a man, woman and child, almost no one was left now who was not screaming and begging for the mercy of God. The train had been rocked significantly by the last wave. O'Leary had seen it coming at the last second and had grabbed for Cap as he fell back onto the ground of the great train to take some shelter from the hit.

Feeling, rather than seeing O'Leary grab for him, Robert too had tried to take shelter from the impending blow. Both men escaped the full brunt of the hit, but their train could not. Never certain of whether it had or it had not, Shannon O'Leary was positive at that moment that the great train had been lifted on to two wheels by the push of the wave. O'Leary looked sharply at his friend. Robert met his eyes as the train continued to ramble slowly down the tracks. "That last wave must have been at least five to seven feet high, Cap!" The awe and fear were expressed clearly in his shaken voice. "And we haven't even gotten over the open water yet..." The dire unspoken fear of the statement hung between them. They were still considered "inland" for the Keys. They still had a great deal of territory to cover where they would not only be closer to the water, but they had a lot of territory to cover where they would be completely exposed over the open water, unprotected by any land!

Suddenly, almost seeming as if he was possessed by demons, Robert jumped up and began working at the controls. "We need more speed!" O'Leary stood up slowly behind him with a mixed look of fear and confusion on his face, as he pressed his back hard against the cold, comforting steel of his engine.

"More speed?!? Have you gone mad man? We don't need more speed. We need to stop this train and get back to the safest speck of land on this tiny, little piece of crap island and ride this thing out! We haven't got a chance out there anymore."

The captain spun back to face his comrade, "Work your fires, Goddamit!" He practically snarled as he bit off the words in his mouth. "We're all dead! It doesn't matter where we go. We're dead now, boy. Don't you get it?!?" The captain's face was contorted in a fit of rage and anger. He looked at O'Leary and the world seemed to slow for a minute. "We're all dead, Shannon." His face relaxed and his voice dropped. "We've failed. We're all dead..." The captain's left hand still clasped one of the controls tightly that he had used to fuel more speed in the engine. Now though, it relaxed. He let it slide limply from the cold iron to fall useless at his side. He looked at Shannon O'Leary with defeat in his eyes. "We've failed." The words fell flat and lifeless from his lips. O'Leary couldn't even hear them. He only saw them as his lips formed them.

O'Leary slowly turned and looked to his right, away from the captain. Something about his gaze and the look on his face told the cap that something big was happening. Robert followed his gaze and turned toward his left where O'Leary was looking. He almost felt his whispered words more than heard them.

"Open water..."

Both men gazed outward as the train moved along faster than it had been, but still nowhere near their typical cruising speed. The world had lightened up a bit as they had moved into open land on either side, unencumbered now by the trees that had only just recently blocked their view. The beautiful blues of the crystal-clear Key waters had been made mad with white caps and ugly by nature.

But it was out there. A few trees passed by still, but they were closer to the water now. They could smell the salt getting stronger through the downpour of the rain. The grounds to either side were almost entirely replaced by water.

"We're still too far away." The captain was talking to himself, but O'Leary was listening. "We should still be inland. We should not be seeing water yet."

O'Leary slid another step closer to his partner. "We are inland cap. There's just no inland remaining." The captain turned to look at O'Leary.

"Hey..." O'Leary looked up at Robert. Robert held his eyes for a moment before he started laughing and said, "We never should have left that last stop."

O'Leary looked at his boss with wonder in his eyes. "Are you going mad? Or are you finally just admitting to being wrong about something?"

"Isn't that the same thing?" Now the captain was starting to laugh like a man who no longer cared where he was. Tears rolled down O'Leary's face as he started to laugh as well.

"Yeah. Maybe staying there would have been the better option." Now they were both laughing loudly. The screams behind them continued as waves began crashing heavily against the sides of the train again. O'Leary turned again and looked back at the water. "I think this might be it Captain."

"I think..." Robert stopped speaking as his mouth stopped forming words. He stared with a mixture of awe and terror at what was growing now right in front of him. The waves were still coming, but now he saw something even worse. He saw death coming for him. He saw waves of 8 and 10 feet in height bearing down upon him. But beyond that, he saw something he had never seen before. It felt like it was taking hours for it to form and move toward him, but he knew it could not have been more than minutes, perhaps even seconds. The wave that was growing behind the others was something like he had never seen before. It was easily three times the height of any man he had ever seen. It blocked out all else in that direction. The world disappeared from view as the wave approached the train, easily outpacing any speed that they could have managed with their puny steam engine, even had they been moving at top speed on a sunny, glorious day.

Robert turned and looked back at the train that trailed behind them. He could not see the people through the walls of the great steam engine that blocked his view, but he could hear them. Over the noise of the great locomotive and the pounding of the storm, he could hear them all. He could picture them in his mind. Their bodies pressed against one another and pressed again the windows. Looking... Watching... Waiting... Knowing the end was coming. Valiant soldiers and scared women; hardened, awful soldiers who had done terrible things and innocent children who had committed nothing worse than simple pranks. All of them, watching and waiting...

Some of the smarter, less-terrified soldiers would be trying to organize them. They would be trying to move people to the right side of the train to help counteract the punch of the water when it hit them. Others would just be cowering on the floor, begging their creator to be merciful and forgive them their sins. He turned back to the wall of water and knew he was none of those. He was not valiant, but he was not terrified. He was not evil out of necessity or basic nature, but neither was he innocent. He was just a simple man, with no one to pray to. God had abandoned him long ago, and perhaps he had done the same in return. He couldn't even remember anymore who had turned away first, him or the man upstairs. In the end though, it no longer mattered.

The water reared up above the toy train now and both men craned their necks to look up at the water as it prepared to fall in upon them. Robert heard the words slowly drip from O'Leary's lips as he prayed his words to whoever would hear them up above. The rain drops actually seemed to stop for a moment as the water above made a cocoon of coldness that protected them from the insanely constant dripping of the rain waters. Robert Walker smiled a small, sad smile for a moment, his tears no longer those of madness, and then shut his eyes as the giant wave attacked.

8:20 PM, Monday, September 2nd, 1935

Landfall of the Labor Day Hurricane

"But... I don't understand." Amy stuttered as she tried to find her words. "If Julie didn't tell you where we were, then how did you know?"

Shelby exchanged sad glances with Tally. Amy was too shocked to see and understand the look, but Jason knew. Amy had mentioned Julie's name many times. Shelby, and even the "slower" Tally, both had come to realize by now that Julie was never going to be found alive. They doubted that the young woman would ever be found at all. They realized that Jason knew this too, but they could tell that Amy was not willing to accept the inevitable yet. She was still in denial. Jason could clearly see that they were trying to figure out how far they should push Amy at this point. Obviously, they decided she wasn't ready yet. "No dear," Shelby began tenderly, "your friend did not tell us. Like I said before, we haven't seen her. Yet..." Shelby caressed Amy's arm lightly as she tried to leave her final word out there for Amy's benefit.

"It was actually Jason's parents who told us that you might be out here." Shelby nodded in Jason's direction without ever taking her eyes from Amy's. "They were trying to reach anyone out here that would answer a phone, cb or a pair of coconuts." Shelby tried to smile at her little joke, but neither Amy nor Jason were interested.

"I guess, they realized that they were never going to get out here in time to help or find you kids. The roads were all blocked and choked with rains. They said they were ten minutes outside of town when they turned around and tried a different tact. That was when they started calling every building out here. Pretty easy to do I guess, since there aren't too many buildings out here on this side of the island. And, most of the lines were down to the few buildings that were still standing." Shelby stopped and this time did look directly at Jason. "Your mother must be very stubborn. She must have tried for an extremely long time before she finally raised us on the cb."

Jason smiled weakly at her. He knew he owed his mother a very, very big hug when he got home.

"Anyhow, she probably tried every frequency possible until she got us. I didn't even know that anyone was out here. I thought they were nuts. I didn't even think a car would have been able to make it out here at the time she was talking about, but this one here," Shelby jerked her thumb over her shoulder at Tally, "wouldn't take no for an answer."

She looked fondly back over her shoulder at Tally. "He insisted that we go looking. Or more precisely, that *he* go looking. I wouldn't go out in this storm on a crazy, wild-goose chase. Imagine my surprise when he came back and said that he had seen a car rolled off the road a ways down. Well, of course at that point, I was more than willing to believe the crazy idea that someone might be out there. That was when... Well. That was when we decided to try the old back-up generator building."

Shelby looked down at her feet. She appeared ashamed of something. Tally stepped forward and put his hand on her shoulder. She flinched, before putting her hand over his as if to thank him for his support. "I wish..." She choked again for a moment before struggling to continue. "I wish we had gone looking for you earlier. Maybe…"

Jason's haze disappeared now. Now he knew what she was choking on. "Ma'am. It wasn't your fault. We were trapped here long before you came looking for us. We sat in that shed for quite some time. My parents would have had to get in touch with you…" Jason paused for a moment and looked at Amy who appeared unfazed by the conversation. "Well. Let's just say that you would have had to have been way earlier to make a difference. We're just happy that you came along when you did."

Shelby smiled slightly and then shook her head. "Thank you for saying that."

Jason smiled the same sad smile. "No. Thank you for saving us."

8:22 PM, Monday, September 2nd, 1935

2 minutes after landfall of the Labor Day
Hurricane

The weight was crushing. It felt like it would never end. Robert couldn't see. He couldn't move. He tried over and over to raise himself up, but there was no use. His lungs burned. His body ached. He tried rolling onto his side. He tried pushing up with his hands and his elbows. He bounced back and forth, sliding one way and slamming into the wall to his left when he got pushed that direction. Everything hurt. He was on the brink of giving up when the weight finally drained off of his chest. He forced his eyes open, forced his mouth open to take a deep, rasping breath and found himself staring up yet again into the big, round raindrops that had resumed falling onto his face.

They suddenly felt much softer in comparison to the anvil that had just leveled him and everything else in its path. Had he not been in so much pain and agony, he may have laughed remembering how earlier he thought the raindrops were "stinging" as they pelted him. Now they felt like blessings compared to the angry wall of water that had treated his body like an infant's ragdoll.

Robert blinked a couple of times to clear his eyes. It was a shock. He coughed and rolled to his side. Spitting out the salt water that he had ingested while under the crushing wave, he looked over towards O'Leary and saw him lying on his back. He appeared to be breathing, but he wasn't moving. Robert struggled to stand up. But putting even that small amount of pressure on his ribs and legs, however, brought immediate, blinding pain to his head. His back spasmed horribly causing him to fall backwards to the ground that he had only managed to get a few inches away from. He squeezed his eyes closed tightly trying to control his agony. He brought his hands to his face and clawed with his fingers as he screamed. Strangely, as he screamed, he noticed for the first time now that other people were screaming as well. Dropping his hands back to the solid, metal floor below him, he stopped for a second to listen, forcing himself not to scream so that he could hear the others. The screams were agonizing. Before they had only been screams of terror. Now they were screams of terror, but there was the wailing of despair and pain as well; horrible, agonizing pain!

Pushing on the black, iron floor one more time with his hands to try to raise himself up, this time Robert rolled to his left taking some of the pressure off of his aching lower back. Although this helped a bit, this time he felt a sharp pain in his right leg specifically. He hadn't felt this before. Looking down toward his shin, he almost threw up as he saw what was hurting so bad. The pain seemed to intensify a thousand percent as his brain registered the impossible angle of his leg. He knew immediately that it was broken. And broken badly!

Closing his eyes tightly, he tried to push out the pain. He had to stand up. He could hear passengers screaming and crying. He had to get out there and help whoever he could. Grunting as he pushed himself all the way up this time to a semi-standing/sitting position, his grunt turned to a scream as the agony of the shooting pain washed over his entire being. Forcing his eyes open, he grabbed on to the side of the train and tried to stop his agonizing screams. Slowly he ground the skin of his forehead against the top of the train railing as he made himself turn his head to look out toward the back of the train. What he saw, finally made him forget his pain. Only momentarily, but it was without a doubt one of the most heart-wrenching sights that he had ever seen. Or ever would see.

The train was splayed out in front of him like a garden snake that had been chopped up into parts and left where it had died. The only part of the rescue train that he could see that remained on the tracks was the engine where he and O'Leary lay. The rest of the train had been swept right off the tracks. The train lay in four separate sections now. All of the cars were still close together, but they were completely separated from their couplings in three areas.

The car that had been connected directly to the rescue engine was now the furthest from the tracks. It was as if it was the end of a tail of rope that had been whipped out wide. Almost all of the cars, other than the engine, lay on their sides. The second to last car was almost still standing, but it was still at an awkward angle, with the roof almost touching the ground. The last car was difficult to see from where he was as it was slanting behind the car in front of it, but it too seemed to be tilted at a bad angle.

As his eyes scanned the wreckage, he immediately realized that he had no hope of helping anyone. The distance was too great, the ground too wet and the rain never ending. Even had he been on two good legs, he would have been near useless to the few survivors that he could see. Watching in horror, he saw bodies moving inside of the train cars, and even some on the ground as well. Most of them were not moving quickly, and with the rain obscuring his vision, it was tough to tell if they were men or women. One thing was for sure, none of the children could have survived. There had not been many on the train fortunately, but the few that were there must have been either swept away by the wave or had been crushed. Robert knew that there was no way their small frames could have survived the crush of the water or the trauma of the crash.

The wailing continued from across the way from the few survivors who still had the energy to cry. It was not as loud now, and the rain seemed even louder, as if it was trying to drown out the horrifying sounds, but he could still hear it as he allowed himself to slump back to the floor of the train. O'Leary moaned softly as he moved on the floor a few feet away from Robert.

Robert moved his eyes in a robotic manner toward his friend. He had no ability left in his body to feel anymore. He was numb all over. His gaze came to rest on his friend's motionless body. O'Leary didn't make any more noise. He was not moving again. As Robert stared at his friend's back, the tears started to flow. Mixed with the rivers of rain water that ran over his face, no one would have ever known that he was crying. They were silent tears against the wailing of the injured and dying, and the pounding of the rain. He let his head fall back against the solid wall and screamed. No one listened to him. He shut his eyes and banged his head against the wall. No one was coming. They were all alone.

8:30 PM, Monday, September 2nd, 1935

Camp #5, Lower Matecumbe Key

10 minutes after landfall of the Labor Day
Hurricane

"I'm telling you, the storm is passing," said
the youngest soldier in the room with them,
again! He had been repeating this same,
annoying mantra for just about the whole time
they had been cooped up in the room. Happily,
though, for the first time all night, Bill actually
agreed with the kid.

"Hey." Bill spoke quietly at first. "Hey!"
This time he raised his voice, grabbing everyone's
attention. "I think newbie might be right this
time." The young kid winced at the annoying
nickname. He hadn't liked it before they had
gotten stuck in this mess and he hated it even
worse now. It wasn't even intended as an insult,
it was just what they called the latest workers to
hit the islands, and yet it still grated on the kid.

"I know I'm right, *boss*." The kid's response showed his annoyance clearly as he emphasized what he considered to be the derogatory nickname for his superior. And he was rewarded with the soul satisfying proof that he was indeed correct.

Bill shot the kid a dirty look. He did hate the boss moniker, almost as much as, if not more, than the kid hated being called newbie. And he did see it as derogatory. Bill hated being older as much as the kid hated being the "new" guy. Still..., it was quiet in the room. The storm continued to rage all around them, but now it sounded more like any other tropical storm that might have bombarded their little spit of land on any other typical day. The rain still slashed and the thunder still rumbled, but it was different now. It was less fierce. It felt less... deadly.

Bill's gaze had been looking upward, as if he could see or sense through the roof whether or not the storm was abating, but now he dropped his head and looked around the room. He let a small smirk of a smile come unbidden to his mouth. He knew it was not a time to smile. How could he allow himself to rejoice when so many had been lost? But he couldn't stop himself. They too could have been dead. They too could have been swept out to sea. But they weren't. They were alive. They had survived. There would be time for grieving for their fellow soldiers and friends later.

But right now, he couldn't help but smile. Neither could his comrades. They were going to live!

9 PM, Monday, September 2nd, 1935

40 minutes after landfall of the Labor Day Hurricane

The conductor, Marcello Vitelli, stared forlornly at his time piece. 9 PM on the dot. He had promised people in each of the cars that he would give another update at 9 PM. He had known at that time that nothing would be different by this hour. Just as he had known the same thing at 6:30 PM, 7 PM and 8:00 PM when he had made his original updates that he had promised people. What he had found over the years though, was that it gave people something to look forward to, some small glimmer of hope that they could pin their expectations and wishes on. He almost felt guilty making the announcements. He knew they were pointless, but the people seemed to get excited for them nonetheless. He was pretty certain that most of them knew they were pointless too, but still, it was better than nothing.

In the end, it didn't even make sense to promise an update at a certain hour. What was the likelihood that any kind of an important update would happen to fall exactly on the hour like that? He was telling them in advance by the very nature of the structured times for his announcement that there was no chance that it would be meaningful at all. If there were any news to be announced, it would be rather obvious from the movement of the train that 'they were leaving', or by the fact that they were being asked to get off the train because it would 'not be leaving'. And, even if the news was not obvious, if there was something to report, he would dare not hold onto it until the appointed hour. Especially if it was good news! Yet there he was, standing in the first car with all eyes on him at 9:02 PM.

Taking a deep breath and releasing it slowly, he broke the bad news again. Four announcements on the hour or the half hour, and four announcements of nothing that mattered!

He tried to spice each one up with some made up or partially true information about how they were getting reports of "things" that they were doing to try to prepare for their departure. But it was all fluff. He literally knew nothing more than they did.

The only good news was that people were no longer angry or demanding action. Now they were just miserable. But at least they were a 'quietly' miserable lot now.

He was on his fourth car full of disappointed and quietly, subdued, angry passengers when he finally got the most incredible news. They were getting ready to move. He was about to inform the remainder of the cars, when he realized that it was a moot point. Word spread like wildfire as the passengers began cheering and yelling to one another. Looking around with a bewildered look for a moment, his face broke into a smile as he abruptly turned and made his way back through three more railcars full of joyous people. Many of the faces showed relief as much as they showed joy. Some just demonstrated weariness. One young lady even went so far as to spontaneously jump up from her seat and give him the biggest bear hug he had received in quite some time as he moved along down the cars. But most importantly of all, all of them were smiling now.

Unfortunately, though, they did not know it, but those smiles would not remain fixed on their jubilant faces for long.

11:53 PM, Monday, September 2nd, 1935

Over 3 hours after landfall of the Labor Day Hurricane

Marcello tapped his finger impatiently on the train console. The train was stopped. Again! All of the jubilance of earlier in the evening had quickly evaporated and the anger and disappointment of the afternoon reappeared with a vengeance. No one was happy. And Marcello was no exception.

Marcello was an interesting character. He was a study in contrasts. Although Marcello had risen well above any station in life that he had ever anticipated obtaining, it had cost him plenty to do so. This was evidenced by his worn fingers and the dirt under his nails. His fingers and palms were scarred and bruised from years of work and toil in all different manner of jobs. He had struggled for many years to get to where he was. During the early 1900's, the relatively young country had struggled to survive a number of small recessions that threatened to bury Marcello and many of the people he knew. Nowhere near as devastating as the recession that they would later experience which would eventually become known only as "the Great Depression," these 'minor' depressions were nevertheless extremely painful for the poor, common people such as himself. Truth be told, nothing about these depressions felt 'minor' to them.

Marcello, however, always viewed himself as a warrior. A driven man who would not let anything hold him back. These depressions, just like the later one he would have to live through, were merely tests to make him stronger and more grateful for what he had.

Eventually though, even as optimistic as he was, he too was on the verge of thinking that everything was for naught. All of his struggles seemed in vain, and each of his endeavors, destined for failure. And just when everything seemed at its bleakest, that was when the breaks finally started to go his way. It had taken years of working insane hours, multiple jobs a day, when he could get jobs, and years of eating less than he should have in order to take care of his health.

But he had survived. Only a young man when the depressions had first begun, he had sworn to himself that he, and his family, would never be in that position again.

Studying to become a conductor and eventually even obtaining the title of engineer had once been an unthinkable dream for him. Trains had become wildly popular in the 1860's before gliding in and out of popularity between that time and the end of the Great Depression. But Marcello had never wavered in his love for trains. They both fascinated and amazed him. Their immense size and power awed him. Still, no matter how much he wanted to get a job in the rail industry and how hard he worked, getting a job on Henry Flagler's premier rail line, the Florida East Coast Railway, had always been nothing more than a pipe dream for Marcello. Or so he had thought.

One lucky day and one chance meeting was all it had taken to turn his life upside down in the most remarkable way. And he had nearly missed his chance. Marcello was the son of Italian immigrants who could barely speak a lick of the

English language and who had suffered greatly to get him across the ocean. They saw America as a chance for their son to get better than what they had. And that lucky day turned out to prove them right.

The year was 1905, and although the worst of the economic problems now seemed to be behind them, after 3 or 4 economic downturns, as he had heard educated people call them, Marcello never felt secure again. He had just finished working a double shift and he was sitting on a bench looking over information about a new locomotive that was supposed to be released in the next few years, when a stranger sat down beside him on the bench. Marcello was vociferous in his reading. He believed with every fiber of his being, that he needed to know about every new invention and every new miracle of engineering that was coming out on the lines at all times. He knew that one day he would have his chance to step up as an engineer and that when that day came, he had to be ready. It was all he thought about.

Whether it was the difference in railroad track width or the ever-increasing speed of the newer model trains, the "what" did not matter. The only thing that mattered was that *he* was the master of knowing it all.

Today's second shift hadn't been about the money, even though in that day and time, it was *always* about the money. It usually wasn't however with Marcello. He worked as a porter at times, despite having attained the position of conductor, simply so he could get more hours on the train and learn more about what made his industry so special. The extra money certainly did not hurt and was always vitally important, but he really just wanted to know everything he could about the industry in order to improve himself.

Why did the people complain when they were on his trains? What did they complain about and to whom did they do their complaining? Who did they complement and why? How much different did the train feel for the passengers back in the Pullman cars when the engineer and conductor picked up speed on certain areas of the tracks? Marcello truly believed that anything that he could learn about the trains could only help him. He also believed that the best place to hear what was really happening amongst the passengers was by being amongst the passengers. And the only way to do that was to be a porter.

Being a porter, however, he stood out like a sore thumb. The majority of the porters were poor, and despite his recent rise in station, that was still no problem for him there. He still looked and truly was poor. But the other discerning factor of most porters of the time was that they were colored folks. George Pullman, who was best known for the Pullman car which was named after him when he became famous for popularizing the famous Pullman sleeper car, began hiring only colored people in the late 1860's, shortly after the civil war had ended. He was so successful utilizing the newly created, cheap labor market that almost every one of his competitors quickly began to copy the concept.

The porter of Marcello's day was not a paid position. They survived and lived off of tips offered by their riders and therefore, theoretically, the better their service, the better their compensation. Because colored folks at the time were so poor and desperate for money, along with the fact that they were accustomed to obeying orders and acting in a docile manner, they were perfectly suited for the position. Even if they were able to get work elsewhere, it's not like they were going to be paid much for it. So, why not work at a job where your own sweat equity could increase your profit? And because they needed it so much, they did work significantly harder than anyone else willing to take the position.

Marcello though, never had a problem getting good tips. He was always one of the most attentive porters on any train that he worked. And he always listened to see why other porters were getting rewarded, or more importantly, why they were being denigrated. Then he stored it away in his brain, so he would know what worked and what didn't.

Unfortunately for Marcello and his attempt at concentrating on his studies, the man who had sat down next to him began speaking. Annoyed that the rude gentleman could not see that he was in the middle of important learning, but brought up by his parents to be polite and respectful, Marcello replied to his questions in short but civil tones. As the conversation went on, Marcello noticed something odd about the questions. Marcello fought hard to keep the words on the small pamphlet in front of him from swimming as they normally did when he was so tired. All he wanted was to close the pamphlet and rest his eyes, but he knew that wasn't possible. He had so little time to study, that every moment was precious and could not be wasted. And now he had this eccentric fellow sitting next to him peppering him with questions.

He had not even raised his head to look at the odd fellow who was seated next to him at first, but now he did. Something about the questions was bugging him, but now he was struggling to even remember what the fellow had asked him about. He had been so focused on not paying attention to what the man had been asking him that he had totally missed the line of questioning.

Squinting at the man next to him as he leaned a little away from him in order to take more of him in, his eyes suddenly widened a bit. Something was definitely not right about this man. "I'm sorry, sir. Who did you say you were?"

The man smiled gently and replied, "I never did." He paused for a moment and then continued. "So how close are you?"

"I'm sorry..." Marcello was confused by the question. Obviously, this was in reference to something they had been discussing earlier that he was not even aware of.

The man smiled patiently. "I do apologize. I know you are trying desperately to study your important notes and I am distracting you, but I am intrigued. You were telling me that you are not far from taking another step toward becoming an engineer. That is quite impressive."

Marcello understood now. "Ah yes. Um, quite close, in fact." Marcello briefly dipped his head and shook it for a minute trying to clear the cobwebs from his mind as he now tried to shift gears and make himself focus on the conversation at hand, instead of his studies. "I have spent double the time of most trying to realize my goal of the engineering designation and promotion due to the fact that I must work my other two jobs and because my reading is not so good. I taught myself," Marcello sheepishly put his head back down again as he was embarrassed by his lack of money and education, "with help along the way from some very generous and wonderful people."

"Remarkable! You must have quite a good deal of drive to be able to push yourself so."

"Well," Marcello put his head down again but this time in a show of deep humility and bashfulness, "I have a very good reason to push myself so hard." His voice dropped in volume. "There is a young lady that I wish to pursue one day, but I do not feel myself worthy of approaching her yet. One day though," he looked up now at the man with a fire and intensity in his eyes, "one day I will be very worthy! Plus," he went on more mildly, "I must make my parents proud. They sacrificed everything for me and my younger brother and I will not fail them. I owe them everything!"

The man who sat next to him held Marcello's eyes now with an extraordinary power as they judged him. Marcello suddenly realized that he was being tested for something, judged by this man for a specific purpose.

"Would being the conductor for that *crazy man* Henry Flagler's railcars be something that might make your parents proud? Something that might make you *worthy* of approaching your young lady friend?" The man winked playfully at Marcello.

Marcello's eyes widened, and his face reflected the surprise and the answer which was clearly written across his face. Tears began to flow from his eyes. He knew that it wasn't possible, but he started to realize that perhaps this could be true. He knew that this man did not belong on this bench next to him. He spoke to Marcello with an air that told him that whatever this man said was not only to be believed but to be trusted without cause for concern. He knew something was different about him.

He looked up and down at the man and studied his clothes more closely. For the first time, his befuddled mind saw clearly what was sitting blatantly in front of him all along. His clothes were clean and pressed and made out of very high-quality fabric. His shoes were carefully polished and well kept, seemingly unaffected by the dust and dirt that blew around in the area where they sat. His fingernails were perfectly manicured, and his hands appeared soft from lack of hard labor. Marcello looked down at his own dirty hands for a moment and saw none of what he saw on the hands of the man in front of him. "Yes, Marcello," the man answered his unspoken question, "you can trust what I ask of you."

Looking up with wonder in his eyes and a smile on his face, he answered with a thrill in his voice. "Without a doubt, sir! Very worthy, sir!"

The man reached out his hand for Marcello's. Marcello looked back down at his dirty, filthy hands and paused. The man looked down at Marcello's hands immediately understanding his concern. "Ah... Never would it be said that I would not shake an honest man's hands because they were dirty due to an honest day's efforts."

Marcello slowly reached out to shake the older man's hand. His firm grasp, even though he was much older than Marcello, reassured everything he had already come to believe about this stranger.

"Come by my office first thing on Monday morning. I will see to it that everything is taken care of for you. You will not be working two jobs any longer, you will earn your new engineering title quickly and you will be on your new train soon."

Marcello could scarcely believe his ears. "But... but sir. I do not even know who you are. Or what office I should report to."

The man had already stood up and slowly begun to move away. Partially turning back to Marcello, he looked at him with a grin. "Sure you do, Marcello. Without a doubt, someone there will be able to tell you where to find Mr. Flagler's office."

"Marcello!" The engineer on the train was practically shouting at him now, forcing him to come back to the present. "Hey! Are you even listening to me?"

Marcello's head snapped up and he looked at his friend in surprise. "What?"

Graziano shook his head. "I knew you weren't paying any attention to me. I said, get back there and try to keep their spirits up."

Marcello shot a look in the direction back to the cars behind him. Looking back at Graziano with an incredulous visage he replied, "What for? We aren't going anywhere!" Gesturing forward, he went on bitterly, "Look at this mess. We won't be off of the Keys by Friday at this pace, let alone tonight or tomorrow."

Graziano smiled grimly. "Of course not, but you offered to do Conductor duty tonight, so..."

Marcello grimaced and put his head down as he shook it back and forth in his manner that he did when he was displeased. And if truth be told, that was not truly a very frequent occurrence. Marcello had the patience of a saint on most nights, but this was certainly not, most nights. It was already very clear to both men that they had no chance of completing this ill-fated trip. They were moving slower than Marcello could ever remember moving on a train for such a long distance. And they hadn't even gotten to the outer edges of the really bad stuff yet.

The clean-up crew in front of them was stopping every few yards to remove debris from the tracks. It had gotten so bad over the last few moments that the crews were no longer even bothering to get back onto the train as it was easier just to walk from one pile of debris to the next.

Not only that, but the size and difficulty of the removal was getting progressively worse with each occurrence. Closer to the main depot from where the train had originally departed, the debris had been primarily small stuff. Occasionally there had been a larger branch or tree that had fallen across the tracks, but for the most part, the early going was fairly easy. As they moved off of the main island though, the level of difficulty increased very rapidly.

Whereas previously, one or maybe two rail workers had been sufficient to remove fallen obstacles, now it was requiring three or even four men, sometimes having to work together in order to get the rail completely cleared. There were one or two very small stretches where they had been able to move freely without much issue, and despite the waves still being large when they passed over it, the bridge between Big Coppitt Key and Upper Sugarloaf was passed rather quickly. After Sugarloaf and Summerland Key however, they went right back into crawl mode. Ramrod, Little Torch and Big Pine were near impassable at parts. Many times throughout the night, Graziano and Marcello were on the verge of throwing up their hands and ordering the train to retreat, when suddenly they would get a break and they would be able to move forward fifty or one hundred yards quickly. Unfortunately, the adrenaline-fueled euphoria would always last for only a few moments at a time. For without fail, the next major roadblock would quickly rear its ugly and disheartening head around the next disastrous corner. Each tease of the end of their misery only served to weaken their resolve even more. But by the time they chose to turn again, again they would be faced with another false hope. And each time they resolved not to go any further, they would shake their heads and say to themselves, but we've come so far to turn around now. And what alternative do we have?

Continuing to drive themselves and their workers beyond the point of exhaustion, nerves completely wrecked, they worked throughout the night. Each man was given a small window of time to get some sleep between shifts. Some of the younger, stronger men who were passengers on the train were also now out on the tracks helping to clear the way for the ill-fated, stranded passenger train.

As the dawn began to appear over the trees that remained standing and the dark shapes that they were working on doggedly in the dark to remove began to crystallize into form, they stopped momentarily to take stock of where they were.

The crazy thing was, Marathon Key, the tiny spit of land that was made up of Boot Key, Vaca Key, Crawl Key, Grassy Key, Big Pine Key, Spanish Harbor and the city of Marathon itself, was essentially unaffected structurally by the storm.

Most of the buildings on these small keys were left intact. Many of them suffered some small structural damage, but nothing that would cause them to be unusable. The landscape though was a different story. Much like all of the other areas, the tracks had plenty of branches and other garbage strewn across them that would restrict their progress. They would later learn that there had been a significant loss of life in this area, relative to the small size of the population, but at this particular moment in time, the passengers and workers had no knowledge of it, and it held no concern for them. Their only thoughts were of getting home.

The train would end up moving forward only a small amount more as midnight came and went. And Tuesday morning was not destined to bring any good news for the people on that train either. It was decided at one point that a small discovery crew needed to scout the tracks further ahead on foot to see how much progress could be made before afternoon and when the tracks would become easier to clear.

The trio of men set out while the sun was still low in the sky and they seemed to have an air of optimism about them. The day break and the lack of rain seemed to convey a feeling that the worst of it might now be over.

While the exploratory trio was gone however, the reality of their plight showed no signs of letting up for the passengers. The meager amount of supplies that the train vendor had been capable of carrying on board had already been nearing dangerously low levels of reserves. As people now began to wake up and demand breakfast for themselves and their children, the scarcity of their supplies became alarmingly apparent to all. Rationing the food made no difference. By the time the vendor had made it to the back half of the train, there were no sandwiches left and very few snacks as well. Many of the passengers were near rioting conditions when the vendor tried to "save" a few morsels for the people in the back of the train. Some people claimed that there were only negroes in the back and that they would simply have to make due. Others claimed, oblivious to how patently wrong they were, that there would still be plenty left for the other passengers, but that they needed more for themselves. And others simply declared in a blatantly rare show of self-preservation and lack of concern for their fellow passengers that they frankly did not care about anyone else, black or white, young or old.

Some of the passengers in the back of the train even tried to move forward to secure food for themselves upon learning of the dismal status of things. Fights erupted once more as the people they passed who did not try moving ahead got angered that they were being further relegated to the back of the line.

The water coolers were empty, the latrines had long since begun to smell and overflow and small children were way past the point of melting down. Being cooped up inside the train with no means of entertainment had long since served to drive everyone on the train absolutely batty. From time to time, hymns could be heard drifting up to the front of the train from the rear box cars where the colored people did what they could to keep their own spirits up.

To make matters worse, the train now was at a complete halt. They had reached a spot of the tracks that were so badly damaged, that passing over them was simply not possible. Men worked for hours trying to repair the damaged rails. Shouts of anger could be heard drifting back from the sweaty, hungry, thirsty and unhappy men who toiled away non-stop. They were every bit as anxious to get off this spit of land as anyone else.

One of the burly men who was working diligently on the tracks stood up momentarily, stretching his weary muscles. He was wiping the sweat from the back of his neck, as the small amount of drizzling rain that had started again was already beginning to cool him off a bit. He was the first to see the returning expeditionary force that had gone to search for news from up ahead. His face reflected very little reaction as he craned his head upward and opened his mouth to catch some of the larger rain drops that were beginning to fall more rapidly once more. Smiling bitterly, he lowered his gaze and stared at the ground for a second, before lifting it back up to look at the discouraged group of three as they trudged slowly back to the train. Mumbling more to himself as opposed to anyone else, his words nonetheless caused everyone to stop working and look up. "Looks like we'll be headin' back to Key West little sooner than some a y'all might'a been a thinkin'." Spitting on the ground, the gruff man turned and began walking back to the train. Without another word, he approached the side of the train, grabbed the metal poll where the steps led up and swung himself onboard. Once he was gone, no one else moved. No one went back to work. No one said anything. They simply looked at each other wordlessly as if searching for someone to give a better resolution, but they all knew that none was coming.

The decision to head back to Key West was as easy as the unknown, gruff worker had made it sound. The report from the three men was simple and quick. The way ahead was pretty open for the most part, but there was no reason to continue any further when they got half way across the island. The entire set of tracks there were washed out, much worse than what they were currently facing, and they hadn't even completely finished dealing with this washout yet. Plus, although this

Key did not suffer much structural damage, the two buildings that had been wiped out up ahead had the distinctly bad luck for the train to be built right next to the tracks. Now unfortunately, according to the scout party, they were directly on top of the tracks but mostly arranged in a huge heap of lumber and debris that was entirely blocking all access to the path ahead. One of the group even said that he saw a fancy looking bathtub that had obviously come from a wealthy northerner family sitting directly on the tracks, straddling them perfectly as if it had intentionally been placed there in some sort of strangely absurd expression of abstract art.

At the end of the report however, as expected, retreating back to Key West was their only viable option.

9:40 AM, Tuesday, September 2nd, 1935

The morning after landfall of the Labor Day Hurricane

The complaining and grumbling had continued from the passengers throughout the morning and substantially increased to an extremely unhappy crescendo when the people on board felt the train begin to move backwards for the first time. Marcello had flat out refused to warn people this time of what was happening. He feared now for his own safety, and with good cause.

People were starting to get more violent. Arguments and disagreements that were just words before were breaking out into full on fist fights among the passengers now. Some of the disputes were over important issues like food and water, while others were over such petty issues that it was absurdly obvious that the *issues* in question were not the actual cause of the altercations. Frayed nerves had long since become the real culprits for most of the passenger's actions.

As the train moved backwards farther and farther though, something happened. The people on board the train got a glimpse of something far worse than what they were experiencing. Their trip through the hurricane ravaged terrain had been completed up to this point all under the cover of darkness. Now, however, in the cruel and revealing light of day, the desolation was impossible to ignore!

Women covered the eyes of their children and turned their own faces away in horror. Men's faces scrunched up in painful grimaces as they witnessed the destruction. Seven Mile Bridge was nothing except water as far as they could see. Mother Nature had not finished thrashing the waters with her cruelly, vicious winds and high tides.

All around them in the water, they observed the remains of people's lives. Furniture, clothes, entire sections of homes ripped from their foundations or shredded into smaller chunks, floating or bobbing up and down in the swollen, raging sea. One poor woman had the unfortunate luck to turn at the wrong moment and after screaming in terror, fainted at the sight of a bloated body that had momentarily been lodged upon a piece of rebar sticking up from the murky waters. She eventually had to be coaxed back to consciousness by a few of the other bystanders who stood by. She was the perfect warning sign for the other women and children not to try any further to see what occurred beyond the safety of their railcars.

The trip back was almost as long as the trip forward had been. And this time it was completed in quiet sadness and dejection. The sights outside had drawn a pall of silence over the previously upset and discontented passengers. Although still upset and discontent now, most passengers felt it difficult to express their anger out loud after seeing what had befallen the other, less fortunate people beyond their windows.

Darkness had just fallen across the land on yet another long, labored day when the train eventually slunk back into Trumbo Island station. Tired, hungry, wet passengers with no place to sleep, nothing to eat and no way to get home stared vacantly around the deserted station. The porters and other few train personnel who were around had no answers for them. Many of the disoriented and unsettled passengers slept right where they were, too delirious to attempt to find anything better. For those who did choose to get off the train, they passed out throughout the area within the station wherever they could find an open place to lay themselves down and stretch out. For some it was on hard stone benches and for some lucky few it was in a small soft patch of grass that was not a large puddle. Most preferred to be out in the open courtyard area and to be off the train to at least be free of the stench. Nowhere was comfortable though. And the rain continued to fall.

Early, Wednesday Morning, September 3rd, 1935

Two days after landfall of the Labor Day Hurricane

Robert's eyes fluttered open for a moment. He closed them again for a minute, pressing hard against the pain. He knew he had lost a lot of blood, he didn't know how much, but instinctively he knew it was too much blood.

His head throbbed, and his body ached, just as it had throughout the entire night. His neck was sore and created an agonizing feeling as he turned it gently left and right. He had no idea what time it was, but at least some light was beginning to shine over the horizon. His stomach growled at him as it had done every time he had woken up during the insufferable night from hell. He was amazed that his body even recognized the slight pain of hunger over the excruciating pain of so many broken limbs and severe contusions.

His head twitched at an unfamiliar sound. He knew from the location where it came from that O'Leary had finally begun to stir. Robert had not heard a sound from him since he had passed out. Robert had actually given him up for dead, much like he had himself. No one had arrived for them yet, and he couldn't imagine anyone would.

Closing his eyes, he breathed in as deeply as he could, preparing himself to attempt to move. His breath rattled in his lungs and pained him both on the way in and the way out. Squeezing his eyes shut one more time in anticipation of the pain, he forced himself to roll in O'Leary's direction, but only managed to cause himself more pain than he had thought was humanly possible for him to bear. Crying out in agony, he rolled back to where he had been positioned originally. Opening his eyes, he looked up into the bluish skies above. He marveled at how blue the sky looked. It appeared so peaceful and serene. Birds circled overhead, cawing quietly as they hovered. The vultures had not arrived yet, but Robert knew that they would not stay away for much longer. The smell of the accident remained the most overpowering smell in the area, but that would not last long. As the sun crawled across the sky, the heat would soon be beating down on them if the rains continued to stay away as it looked to be the case at the moment. Soon the flesh would begin to rot and the vultures would come. Already Robert could smell, or perhaps it was only that he sensed, the smell of his wounds as they began to dry and crust, inviting infection into his body.

Letting his head fall back in defeat against the floor of the train, he settled in as best he could. He didn't know if he was settling in for the long wait until death would come, or if perhaps by some miracle, he was waiting for a lifesaving rescue. Either way, there was nothing further that he could do, but lay there and listen. He tried to tune out the sounds. He tried not to think about the other people laying out there dying and mourning their family and friends who they had already lost. He tried not to think about his own family and friends who were surely sitting at home, praying for his soul, assuming him lost with the others. As he lay there, praying for a release, a release of any kind, Robert did his best not to think about anything.

9:13 AM, Wednesday, September 3rd, 1935

Two days after landfall of the Labor Day Hurricane

Marcello shook his head sullenly as he looked at the group of four men from the railroad station who stared quietly at him. No one wanted to face the people outside. A few of the forlorn passengers had come forward to ask about arrangements, but the majority of them simply sat dejectedly where they had woken up, and waited, many of them not even knowing what they were waiting for. Others had gone off in search of food, trying to find any establishments that would be able to offer them food or water. Almost all of the passengers were hungry and thirsty.

Marcello looked silently down at the small scrap of paper in his hands. "I'll do it," he paused a beat and then continued sternly, "but this is the last time." He looked up at the men in front of him gesturing emphatically in the direction of the waiting boat, "When I get on that steamer, I become another passenger just trying to get home, just like the rest of those people out there.

No more announcements, no more dealing with disgruntled people. I'm done." He looked each one in the eye, one by one. Each one immediately nodded, grateful to be relieved of the position that Marcello was about to take. The fact that this was the only option open to these people to get them home was not going to make this any easier. These people were not stupid. They would know what lay ahead of them when he laid out the plan in front of him. No one was going to be happy about it.

Without another word, Marcello spun on his heel and pushed out into the beautiful, bright day that was shaping up in Key West that morning. Most people would have loved to have been in Key West on a day like this. But these poor people would have given anything just to have been home.

4:00 PM, Wednesday, September 3rd, 1935

Two days after landfall of the Labor Day Hurricane

For the first time in a long time it seemed, something happened the way it was supposed to. Marcello sat down in one of the very few vacant areas that still remained on the S. S. Cuba. A weight had been lifted from his shoulders now that he was no longer technically in charge of anything. His shoulders slumped as he felt the hum of the engines and sighed with relief as the Peninsular and Occidental Steam Ship Company's steam boat slipped gracefully out of the port of Key West right on time at 4 PM on the dot. It was still headed along its normal itinerary, bound for Tampa, Florida, but this trip was now anything but normal. Packed with the additional passengers of the Labor Day train, they also retained the passengers who would have otherwise disembarked in Key West to take the Overseas Railroad bound for Miami.

The plan was, that upon arrival in Tampa, they would all be transferred to trains that would carry them northeast across the state to connect with the Florida East Coast Railway for the final leg south back down to Miami. Certainly not the straightest possible path for the stranded Labor Day weekenders, but at this point, it definitely appeared to be about the only path available.

Such was the ambitious plan as the S.S. Cuba, overflowing with Cuban and Key West passengers plus their new stowaways, sailed late Wednesday afternoon on what was supposed to be a brief and pleasant overnight cruise to Tampa. Unfortunately, Mother Nature was not aware of how things were *supposed* to go. The Gulf of Mexico was still wildly turbulent in the wake of the hurricane and the journey was anything but smooth. Seasickness was widespread. There weren't enough pillows, blankets, or deck chairs and those passengers who left theirs unattended for any length of time, typically ended up without them when they returned. And although the food was plentiful and well prepared, the seas were rough causing many of the passengers to spend much of their time out on the deck leaning over the railings, leaving much of the delectable food uneaten.

The Cuban and Miami passengers who remained on the boat for the extended cruise were in much better spirits than those who had suffered many nights of misery, as would be expected. But with all of the extra people on board and the cloud of gloom that hung over them, the jovial nature of the original passengers did not last for long.

Wednesday Evening, September 3rd, 1935

Two days after landfall of the Labor Day Hurricane

Robert's eyes fluttered open again. How long had he been asleep this time he wondered? Or perhaps 'passed out' was the better way to phrase it.

He tried to make sense of what was happening. It was darker now. He had woken up at different times throughout the day. At least he assumed it had only been one day. Sometimes it was hot and oppressive. Other times it was cold and rainy. Sometimes he was too dazed and out of it to even register his surroundings. Now however, something different was happening. He tried to make his senses focus. He tried to understand what he was feeling. Shapes were moving around him, he could tell that, but he couldn't determine what shapes. Had the vultures finally gotten around to him? Was it finally his turn under the beak? He didn't feel pain, at least not any more than he did at any other time when he had opened his eyes.

Now it began to register. Now it began to come into focus. He could feel them. They were hands. His body was being gripped by hands. Words were starting to penetrate his consciousness. He tried so hard to respond to them. He wanted so desperately to convey his agony to them. He wanted to tell them how hard he had tried to save his passengers, the people whose lives had been entrusted to him. But try as he might, nothing would come out. His words were choking in his throat. Nothing but rasps and incomprehensible grunts would emerge. His frustration was making it even more difficult. He began crying as he fought to make himself heard and understood. His body was wracked with spasms and convulsions as he struggled with every fiber of his being. Eventually as the blackness closed in on him once more and as his consciousness began to fade again, in his mind he raged against his impotence. He hadn't said a word. He couldn't do anything. He was powerless. Helpless. And then he was gone.

Thursday Morning, September 4th, 1935

Three days after landfall of the Labor Day
Hurricane

Thursday morning started out much better. Most of the passengers no longer had anything left in their stomachs with which to be sick any further. And Mother Nature had finally gotten the message that they had suffered enough. The waters had turned calmer during the night as the storm continued to push further north and to the east of their position. It was now situated somewhere along the western coast of Florida and was pushing northeast at a reasonable speed. There was a good chance that it would be off the peninsula and into Georgia by the beginning of the next day. Nevertheless, all the passengers cared about was the fact that it was no longer in their area and it was no longer giving them further problems.

Coming around the bottom of the coast of Florida and turning north to head up parallel along the same path as that which the hurricane had taken, they were now behind the path of the storm and seemingly out of harm's way. Sailing into the port of Tampa early Thursday morning, many passengers were starting to get the sense that their long, arduous, painful journey might soon be coming to an end. One connection to go on the other side of the state and they could potentially be home by the end of the day.

As the weary and disheveled passengers disembarked in the port of Tampa, sad, mournful gazes met them at the gates. The people of Tampa had already heard about the plight of the Key West and Miami passengers. Despite the phone lines remaining down in the Keys, and very little communication escaping the isolated islands, word had still managed to make it all the way up to their part of the world by various means. In reality, most of the people in Tampa had been watching intently to see if the storm would turn their direction. And although Tampa had once again managed to escape the bull's-eye, it still served to keep them informed as to the misery and destruction of their neighbors to the south.

Tampa, it seems, was a very lucky town with respect to hurricanes. Prior to the relatively weak category 3 Hurricane that had struck the area in 1921, which appeared especially weak when compared to the one that was currently ravaging the peninsula, they had not seen a real hurricane directly hit the area since 1848. And even that one was *not that bad,* all things considered, although that was primarily because there simply weren't that many people or structures in the Tampa Bay area at that time to be killed or destroyed. The storm had significantly changed the lay of the land, which had demonstrated just how bad it could have been, had there been more people and buildings in the area at that time.

Entire land masses had been realigned by the winds and water surges, surges which hit the highest levels ever recorded in that area. Much like the Overseas Railroad had just recently been washed away by the Key's Hurricane, Tampa had had new passes opened and islands split in two by the extreme forces of nature. A hospital and a lighthouse had been completely flattened by the tidal-like waves of the gulf. Pinellas County, the area that was mostly comprised of the small town of Clearwater, had been completely inundated with water. Up to waist deep in many parts, and the two bays had actually met when the land mass was completely submerged.

But that was 1848, almost one hundred years ago. Almost no one was alive who had lived through that day. And this was today. The haunted looks of the survivors staring back at them as they shuffled along through the long lines, moving sullenly to the waiting trains that would hopefully finally deliver them home, struck them vividly. They could only imagine what these people had been through. Whatever it had been, they could only breathe a sigh of relief, as the doors slid shut on the overflowing train cars and pulled out of Tampa, that it had not been them.

Thursday Afternoon, September 4th, 1935

Four days after landfall of the Labor Day Hurricane

Sharon and Tina had not spoken very much since they had made their transfers from the train to the boat and now back again to their latest train. Patty too, was unusually quiet. They were as tired and hungry as everyone else and it showed in their faces and their body language. They moved slowly, and they groaned when they did. Their bones and muscles ached from sleeping and sitting in uncomfortable positions for hours on end. The lack of good food, or food that they could keep down when on the boat, had made disasters of their digestive systems. Nothing seemed to work right for anyone on the train internally. They needed normalcy. They needed their old lives back. They needed off this train!

Sharon raised her head dejectedly as the train came to a stop in yet another small depot, if you could even call it that. It was really more of an empty field as far as she could tell. They had jumped off with most of the other ravenous passengers at the first few stops, desperately invading every little roadside stand, market, restaurant or food vendor they could find. After a few of these piddly little stops, they began to get a better feel for which stops may actually hold the promise of something to eat. It appeared as if they were literally stopping at every tiny station they passed. At some of the stops where she didn't see a soul, Tina wondered if anyone even got on or off.

The cessation of motion got their attention and she moaned quietly giving another small grimace at the latest stop that they immediately wrote off. Tina did not even bother to lift her eyes or head as the train made its now very familiar groans and shudders that indicated that it had settled fully into place. The smoke blew out from its engine and one or two people got on and off. Patty made her displeasure known this time, "This sucks!"

Sharon looked up at her daughter with a weary expression. Patty made eye contact with her mother and had the look on her face of someone who suddenly realizes that they had just made a really awful blunder.

But much to her daughter's shock, Sharon just nodded her assent, leaned her head back against the seat back and closed her eyes. As

Patty's shock wore off and she realized that she was not in trouble for her out of the ordinary expletive, she realized that it did not bring her much joy, and she too lowered her head and found a spot on the floor to stare at gloomily. "How many more stops to make?" She finally mumbled.

"Just a few more hours to go," her mother murmured. "Just a few more hours to go..."

Friday 2 AM, September 5th, 1935

Four days after landfall of the Labor Day Hurricane

The last 270 plus miles that they traveled from the junction north of Miami into the FEC depot in downtown Miami on Flagler Street was absolute hell. And given everything that they had been through up until that point, it was very difficult to say that it was the worst part of the trip, but for many of them, it certainly was.

They had not been able to eat a decent meal throughout the entire trip across the heart of the state. As packed as the train was, most of the passengers did not have enough room to get comfortable and the constant stops and loud noise made any type of meaningful sleep near impossible.

When the train finally coasted to a stop for the absolute last time on their marathon journey, they were exhausted and at wits end. They had started their journey from this very spot 7 days earlier in the lap of luxury on one of the most incredible trains to ever roll across our planet. And they had ended back in this very spot bereft of that luxury. They had traveled in horrible conditions, they had traveled by various means and in the end, they had glided back into the station in a passenger train that was ill-suited for their tastes and their expectations. They had paid $2.50 for a ticket that was supposed to offer them an experience of a lifetime. And it did. Very few of the people who rode that train and who had taken part in this tragedy would ever forget the experience. It was burned into their very psyches.

Sunday 2 PM, November 14th, 1937

Over two years since landfall of the Labor Day Hurricane

Jason stood on the long stretch of narrow highway swaying back and forth stamping his feet on the ground. He had not arrived early enough to get one of the wooden backed chairs that dotted the area in front of the monument draped with the flowing white sheet.

It was cool out and stamping his feet while swaying served to keep him a little bit warm against the biting wind. The sun shone down heavily on his face warming him, but the cold wind bit more fiercely.

It was a stark contrast from the day so many years ago when Henry Flagler's famous train had first coasted into the Trumbo Depot on Key West. Jason of course hadn't been born at that time and had only heard stories of the event, but he knew that there had been a historic heat wave at that time. Ironically, as they sat waiting for the speeches to end 25 years later, they faced just the opposite today. The historic cold spells were sweeping across the nation, even getting all the way down to their little corner of the world.

It was ironic, he supposed, the heat of that first day warming the flames of excitement and anticipation, versus the cold of this day, which accentuated the pain and agony of remembrance with its biting sting.

Raising his hands to his mouth, he cupped them together and blew into them. He couldn't hear what words were being spoken by the dignitaries up front, but he didn't really care either. He hadn't even decided he was coming today until the last moment. His parents had been urging him to show up for it. Jason assumed that they secretly thought that this would somehow be cathartic for him. He was certain it would not be.

He scanned the crowd one more time, but still could not see her in the large group of people. It appeared as if they might have indeed gotten more than 4,000 people here for the event. The papers had reported that it was going to be a big showing, and it certainly seemed to be living up to their expectations.

As he lowered his eyes back down from his fruitless search for Amy, he thought back to that fateful night. He tried as often as possible not to think about it. Many times though, the images thrust themselves into his mind despite his best efforts. Squeezing his eyes shut and begging himself not to envision his two friends dying as he failed to save them again and again. Usually though, it was of no avail. The images always came back, especially the images of Julie.

Rubbing his arms briskly one more time for a quick second, he thrust his hands deep into his pants pockets to keep them warm. As he did, he felt and sensed someone slide up from behind him to his side. Jumping a little bit at the sudden invasion of his privacy, he jerked back a bit at the initial contact. Amy did not seem to react at all to his initial rejection of her touch. Instead, she simply smiled a small, sad smile and gave him a slight bump with her hip. Jason returned the small, sad smile and held her eyes for a moment. Eventually he turned back to the monument and the speakers. Just as he did, the speech appeared to be coming to a somber conclusion. With a great flourish that seemed a bit out of sync with the solemnity of the moment, or perhaps just the lack of understanding of a politician not from the area, who had not lived through the disaster, the white sheet was pulled away.

Jason and Amy both looked upon the simple, white block monument. It looked to be about 20 feet tall and it was made from limestone quarried in the local areas. There was not much to it. In the center was a simple, unsophisticated picture of waves and trees blowing in the deadly, unseen winds of the hurricane. Below it was an inscription that said no more and no less than what was needed. The plaque merely read, "Dedicated to the memory of the civilians and war veterans whose lives were lost in the hurricane of September Second, 1935."

Amy had stood momentarily by Jason's side, neither of them speaking, with her arms crossed, slowly rubbing her arms for warmth. Now she let her hands drop to her side. Her left hand reached out slowly, searching for his. They had not spoken much since the tragedy, but this didn't require much speaking. Jason removed his hand from his pocket and intertwined his fingers with hers. Looking down to her, Amy slowly turned and looked up at him. She spoke quietly and sweetly to him, "I feel like taking a ride out to the beach. You want to join me?"

He smiled at her lovely face as she smiled up at him. "Yeah," he replied. "I think that would be great."

She squeezed his hand and allowed herself to smile a little bigger. "I'm really happy to see you again."

He smiled down at her for a moment, and then he briefly looked back up at the memorial. Pulling his eyes from the large memorial of lives that had passed, he looked back down to his future and to his life that seemed to just be starting again. "Me too," Jason said. "Me too!"

As they turned and walked back to the car, the cold wind at their backs finally seemed to bite a little less cruelly.

Historical Aftermath

Although it is difficult to compare the ferocity of catastrophic weather-related events across different time periods, there are some simple comparisons and statistics that can easily show us how destructive the Labor Day Hurricane of 1935 truly was.

To begin with, the most reliable data that we have today tells us that the Labor Day Hurricane is one of only three hurricanes ever to touch the US coast designated as having "Category 5" hurricane strength.

34 years after the Labor Day Hurricane had forever altered the history of the little string of Key islands, Camille would devastate the mouth of the great Mississippi River with the strongest winds ever recorded. And then, another 23 years after that, Andrew would do its damage to the coast of Florida, taking a route that looked very much like that of the Labor Day Hurricane as it passed over the Caribbean and the southern part of Florida. Andrew passed a little higher in the Keys than the Labor Day Hurricane, touching primarily on Key Largo to the north of where the Labor Day Hurricane had hit, and although the

Labor Day Hurricane remains the hurricane with the strongest maximum sustained winds and the lowest barometric pressure at the time of its landfall, Andrew went down in history as the costliest hurricane of its time for a continental US landing, and as of the writing of this book, the fourth costliest in US history, having since been surpassed in financial disruption by Katrina, Sandy and Ike.

The death toll from the Labor Day Hurricane has been very difficult to quantify in any definitive manner. Part of the problem in identifying the true number of lives lost is that many of the people on the islands were washed out to sea and their remains were never recovered. Coupled with the fact that time was a big factor in trying to prevent epidemic outbreaks, the National Guard had to be called in to assist with saving the living and disposing of the deceased in a manner that would serve to keep the area clear of disease. Disposing of the deceased in a "sanitized" manner meant making use of large funeral pyres and massive common graves.

Still, most estimates have placed the death toll into the range of 400 to 500. The highest estimates have been placed at as many as 800. This includes over one third of the 750 veterans who were stationed at the government camps located on Windley and Matecumbe Keys. Amazingly however, not one person on the rescue train that was derailed ended up dying.

After the horrendous loss of life, the destruction of the Overseas Railway was the next biggest victim. More than one-half of the tracks and infrastructure of the Overseas Extension of the Florida East Coast Railway was lost within that single 24-hour period. It was reported that the land and the bridges were eventually sold to the State of Florida for approximately $640,000 after the stockholders and the government decided that rebuilding was simply not a good fiscal decision. And although the Overseas Railway was a modern miracle by anyone's definition, that miracle never morphed into what it really needed to be in a Capitalist society such as ours, a successful means of making money! In the end, it was not entirely the destructive force of the hurricane that led to the ignoble demise of the on-again-off-again revered railroad. The internal combustion engine was far more devastating to the long-term sustainability of the train than the hurricane ever could have been. The hurricane was merely the catalyst that sped up the undeniable reality that it would one day be relegated to the forgotten annals of history.

Along with the events described within this book, there were a number of other grievous mistakes that led to the disaster of the Labor Day Hurricane. Here are a number of those additional errors not alluded to previously in this fictional account:

Supervisors and workers at the camps on the Keys noticed a large, mass migration of crabs as they moved overland from the Atlantic side of the island chain to the Gulf side. Another group that made the move from one side of the islands to the other was large schools of tarpon that swam from the Atlantic to the Gulf waters. FERA (Federal Emergency Relief Administration 1933 – 1935) officials were told of both of these anomalies for the purpose of explaining how bad the coming storm might be, but to no avail. FERA officials shrugged off the warnings as unscientific and determined that they were not to be taken seriously.

Ignorant of the hurricane's path and developing strength, and confident that a train could arrive in time to assist all of the workers and their families in an evacuation, FERA officials made many blunders as the storm approached the Keys. In a shocking display of heartlessness, bosses on the islands were ordered to confiscate the keys to the many cars and flatbed trucks that could have evacuated workers to Miami and potential safety. And, even more shocking, as the storm raced menacingly towards the Middle Keys, a unit of the National Guard was ordered to set up outside the camp near Tavernier to force veterans to remain at their posts.

The level of miscommunication and poor judgment that transpired between FERA and Flagler's Railroad bordered on the level of criminality because it was so extensive. FERA officials were under the erroneous impression that the train would be prepared to move the moment the request for assistance was made, but railroad officials on the other hand had demands that they expected to be met before they would assist in any relief efforts. What it eventually came down to was a fee of $300 that needed to be delivered before they would even begin to prepare the train. On top of this, no one from FERA even had an accurate idea of how much time would be required to reach the camps. Nor were they aware of what the railroad's plans were for doing so. The majority of the details were eventually worked out when both sides finally got on the phone between Tampa and Miami. Unfortunately, by this time, the situation had for all intents and purposes moved from desperation to a suicide operation, as the Labor Day Hurricane had already begun moving rapidly towards the unprotected camps.

To learn more about the Labor Day Hurricane and its long-lasting effects on the Keys, you should do your best to visit the Keys themselves and stop in to see the Florida Keys History Museum. And if you have the opportunity, the Labor Day Hurricane Memorial is also worth a visit. Both landmarks can be found on Islamorada, a quarter of the way from the bottom of Florida to Key West, or about an hour by car from Homestead, Florida.

Acknowledgements

Special thanks to my dear family and friends who have always supported me in every aspect of my life.

Thanks to Kalani McDaniel for her assistance with editing and ensuring that I know the difference between then and than.

And an extra special thank you to all of the many writers who inspired me to take up this book in the first place. Unfortunately, I do not even know who the first author was who originally inspired me. I was visiting the Keys on a business trip when I went out on my own to explore for a bit. While shopping in a small little 'mom and pop' store right off of Duval Street, I happened to pick up a short 100-page book that described the Labor Day Hurricane and gave details about the bridges that I had driven over on my trip out to the islands. Immediately intrigued, I could not get the idea for a story out of my head. Less than a year later, I could no longer stop myself from telling the amazing story that had been rolling around inside my head for so long.

For whatever reason, the idea of how the hurricane hit and the changes that it left behind simply took hold of me and would not let go. And as I delved deeper and deeper into the story of Henry Flagler and what he did for our state, of which I had not previously been aware, I continued to become more and more engaged. Quite simply, without Henry Flagler and the magnificent Overseas Railroad, Florida would not be what it is today!

About David Siracusa

David Siracusa is a dedicated husband to Fran Siracusa, father of two wonderful kids, Luciano and Giovanni Siracusa and slave to their dog, Elsa. Giovanni takes care of the tortoise, Freedom.

Dave is a successful business owner, running a PEO Brokerage in Clearwater, Florida and considers himself to be a friend to every charity he has ever met. He tries as hard as possible to make his company the best company that any of his employees have ever worked for and he considers them all to be family.

His goals in life are to be happy at all times and to help bring joy to any people that he meets or spends time with, EXCEPT for people whom he plays against on the basketball court. Those people he hopes curse his name as the best defensive player they have ever come across and have never been able to get past.

Finally, he hopes that you enjoyed this book and found the story of the Overseas Railroad's birth and death every bit as fascinating as he did.

Made in the USA
San Bernardino, CA
29 March 2020